UNORDINARY

VOLUME 1

Story & Art by uru-chan

An Imprint of HarperCollinsPublishers

HarperAlley is an imprint of HarperCollins Publishers.

unOrdinary Volume 1

For information address HarperCollins Children's Books, a division of HarperCollins Publishers, 195 Broadway, New York, NY 10007.
www.harperalley.com

ISBN 978-0-35-846778-6 — ISBN 978-0-35-846780-9 (pbk.)
ISBN 978-0-35-861531-6 (signed edition)

Lettering by Kielamel Sibal
Layout design by Lor Prescott, HB Klein, and Chelsey Han
Book design by Celeste Knudsen

23 24 25 26 27 GPS 10 9 8 7 6 5 4 3 2 1

First Edition
A digital version of *unOrdinary* was originally published on WEBTOON in 2016.

Two years ago, my father wrote a book.
It was about a man who lived amongst a world of Zeroes.

This man, he used his ability only for others...

Helping the weak.

Saving lives.

Spreading wealth.

Spoiler: he ends up dying.

But it wasn't sad,

because he brought charity.

And the world became peaceful.

CHAPTER 1

The school's famous Triple Chocolate Cake is only served once a month...

And because this is such a rare event, everyone rushes to the cafeteria first thing during lunchtime.

I always get there late because I'm not as fast as everyone else.

But TODAY, I have a good feeling!

What? You "called it"? You should know how it works by now, Remi.
It's first come, first serve. If you want a piece, you gotta be faster than that!
Better luck next time!

No way. I've waited an entire month for that cake. I won't back down!
Hand it over, jerk!
BZZT
Oh, so that's how you want to play?
Bring it on, Pinky!
LOOSEN

Oh god, those two are at it again...
Really? Ugh, here we go.
BAM!!!

Great, they're already fighting over the last piece.
I'll never get a slice...

MATH CLASS
ow free ou g only right trian be able to work with rts of triangles. we w introducing the law nd the law of cosines ne derivation of thes ws be through the us f right triangles, bu ese laws us put t riangle back
at notat f are, we wi a present th ngth the sides f a triangle while the quantities pha and gamma ill represent e measure
GLOOM~

into the rt with out w e and again we the vertex down have a triangle sim had before. So w he right side to lab gths of the triang ht triangles we ean theorem the le
alpha equals ens then we wo alpha equals ze situation, the law ines simplifies to ared plus b square uared, or in othe Pythagorean the w of cosines c f as a geom
e of th vertexes d s correspond e. Combining t esults with what already have w eave us with the wing, a over s equals b o eta ds
This class sucks.
I live in an ordinary world... and go to an ordinary school.

us eq squared plus quared minus t times b a cosine lgorithm b square equals a squared plus squared minus two t a c cosine beta. C squared quals a squared squared minu cosine

Who wants to come up and prove this law?

RAISE
Can I use the bathroom?
John.

Go ahead.

Whoa, scary...

Hah! Don't die on your way there, Johnny Boy!

WHACK

Mr. Mardin.
Perhaps you'd like to volunteer?

Overall, my life is pretty ordinary...

*Except...HOLY SH*T!*

I could've died just now...

CRUMBLE

Um... h-hey? Are you all right?

stagger
PISSED

Except...
I wasn't born with an ability of my own.

DOWN YET A DIFFERENT HALLWAY
You've gotta be kidding me...
Come on, do that thing again.
No...
L-leave me alone!
BAM!!
Look here.
PULL
DO NOT TALK BACK TO ME!

TILT

Now... do what I say.
Or I'll beat the crap out of you.

?!

BUMP!

THUMP!

Keep your hands to yourself.

Heh.

I know who you are...
You're John, the school zero!

Trying to play hero, huh?
You're pretty ballsy.
CRACK

But you should really know your place!

BLOCK

POW!!
Back off.
You'll pay for that!
WOBBLE

What the hell do I do against **that**?
Haven't you learned?
The world doesn't have sympathy for weaklings like you.
Lay low and mind your own business...
Or keep getting in others' ways and get **killed**.
Was that a threat?

?!

Ugh!
BAM!

He's so fast!
Just now, his skin was rock solid.
Increased speed and durability...?
Oh, I get it!

That was only a taste of what I can do.
If you beg me, I'll let you leave here in one piece.
Seriously? Your ability isn't even that good.
You're just gloating because you finally found someone weaker than you.

Pft...!
HAHAH AHAH!!
What the hell are you laughing at?
You, of course! Beg? That's a pretty big demand.
Usually, when someone talks like that, they can back it up.
Let me give you some examples...

So, we have Remi, who could burn me to a crisp.
Blyke and Isen, who are currently blowing up Wallik Hall.
And obviously, Seraphina, who is pretty much a god.
TAT TAT
Okay, your turn!
What can **you** do?
Move a little faster? Hit a little harder?
Lean
Doesn't seem too threatening...
Snap!
In fact...I bet I could beat you even without an ability.
You...
...SHUT THE F*CK UP!!!
DASH!

GRAB

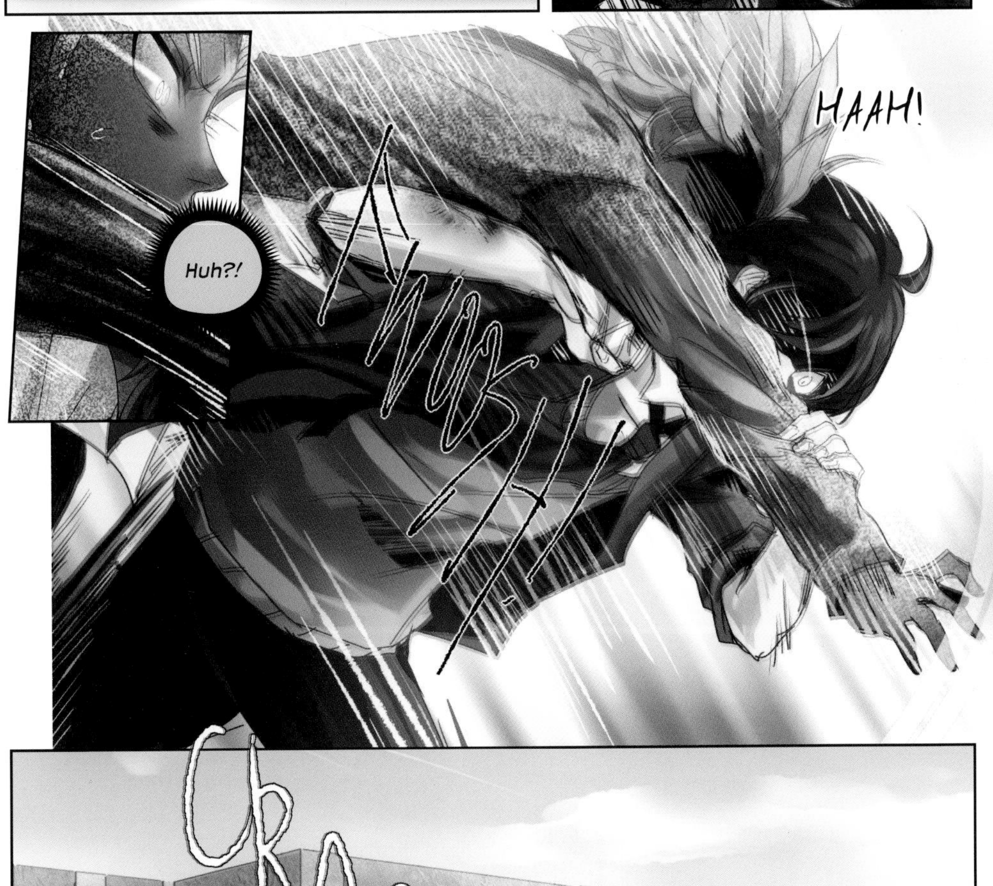
HAAH!
Huh?!
WHOOSH

CRASH!!

Relief
HOLY SH*T!
That actually worked?
Almost pissed myself!

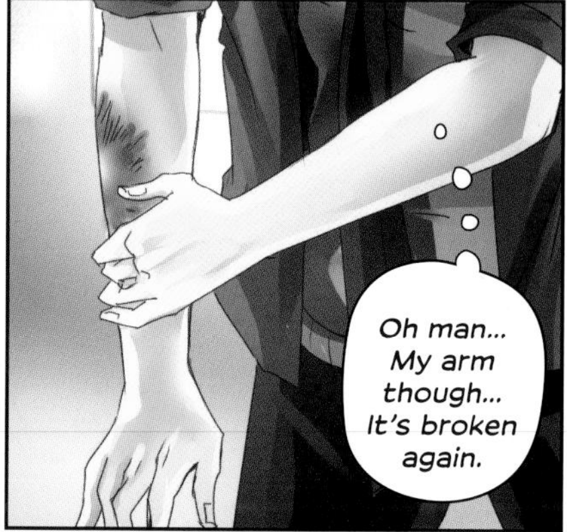
Oh man... My arm though... It's broken again.

SIGH—

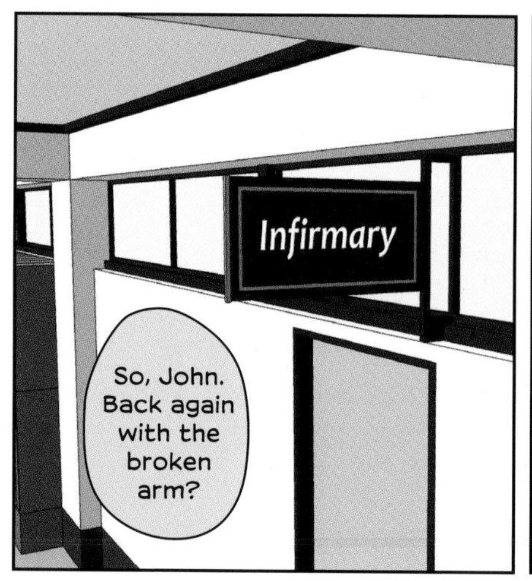
Infirmary
So, John. Back again with the broken arm?

How many times do I have to tell you to watch yourself?

DO YOU REALLY HAVE TO DIE BEFORE YOU UNDERSTAND?
AH! CALM DOWN, DOC! I SAID I'M SORRY!
Here, drink this. Your arm will heal in three hours.
Luckily, you only ran into Stone-boy today...
If you'd pissed off any of the higher tier students...

...then even I wouldn't be able to do much to sav-
I already know, Doc.
Thanks.

Don't worry, I'll be more careful.
Where do you think you're going?
Nice try, but you know the drill.
You're not going **anywhere** until you've healed.
I will notify your teachers that you won't be attending classes for the remainder of the day.

Beep
Beep
Hwelp me im dying1!
Where are you?
. . .

Ugh, not the other one...
CLOSE

John.

Ah, Sera!

What's this about?
You really don't waste any time, do you?

I'm bored. Doc won't let me leave for another three hours!
PFFT
Lol sucks for you

Well, I gotta go back to class.
WHAT?!
But I'll remember to **not** wait for you when school is over. See ya!

Who are you kidding?
Grab

You never go to class.
Come on! Help a friend out! Stay with me.

Sigh

Bing
Bing
Bing
Bing

What's that creepy look for?
Kekekekekekeke
I'M GLAD YOU ASKED.

Check.
This.
!!
Out!!

SlappyPIG
Game Over! :(
score 187
best new! 187
Looks like we got a new champ in town!

Hm, pretty good.
But...still not good enough...

...!!
WHAT? 212?!

You cheated. That doesn't count.
What?

Because I used my ability?
Look, it's not my fault you don't have one...

Rumble rumble rumble
!!

What was that?
YOU HAVE GOT TO BE KIDDING ME!!
Huh?
Bing
bing

JUST WAIT TILL I GET MY HANDS ON THOSE KIDS!!
JOHN.
Glare
YOU WILL STAY HERE UNTIL I'M BACK! IS THAT CLEAR?

Don't worry about me, Doc! I have Sera to keep me company!
Waves
That's what I'm afraid of...

SLAM!!

Hey, Sera...
Let's get out of here.

Sure.

Rustle
rustle

THAT NO-GOOD ZERO!
I'll destroy him the next time I see him!!

Phew!
Woo! Freedom!

Speak of the devil!
RUSTLE!!

GOT YOU, YOU LITTLE B*TCH!

I'VE GOT A BONE TO PICK WITH YOU!

You again?
GULP

Hey, is this about earlier?
Come on, let's forget about it and make up, okay?
YOU THREW ME OUT THE WINDOW!

Yeah? And you broke my arm...so let's just call it even.
SHUT YOUR FILTHY MOUTH!

FWP!
Kuh!

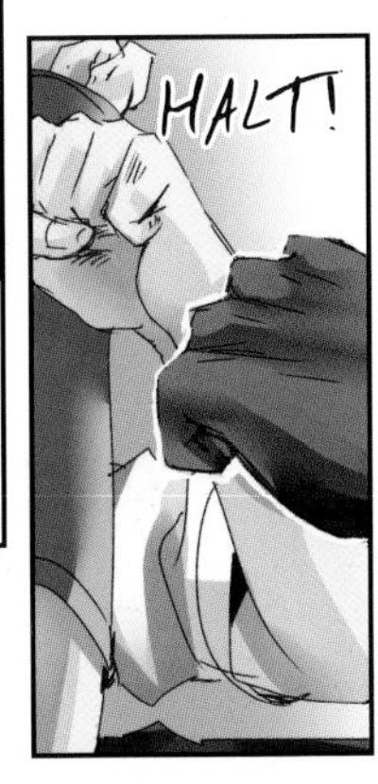
HALT!

?

...

Seraphina?!
SUCK IT!

GLARE—
Stand down.

Am I supposed to be scared?
So, I've heard rumors about you...

But how strong can you possibly be if you hang around this weakling all day long?
Seriously?
SO HOW 'BOUT YOU LEAVE AND MAYB-!

BAM!?!

Don't waste my time.

What the hell?
I didn't even see her move...

Grr...

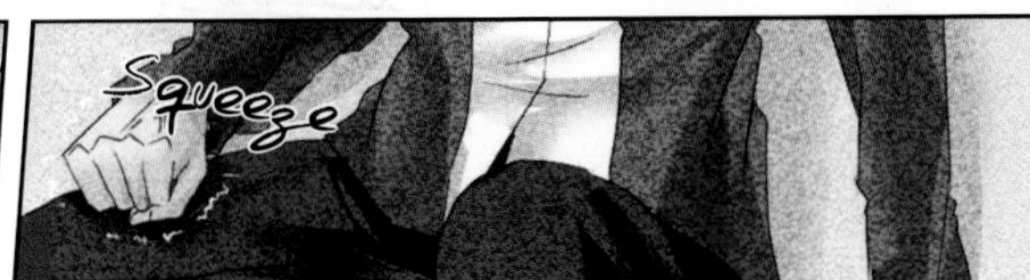
Squeeze

GO TO HELL!
WHOOSH!

BONK!

...

So where did you want to go?

OH RIGHT!

How 'bout a drink?

Sure, but it's on you.
You got it!

LATER BACK AT SCHOOL
We're so screwed...

HOW DARE YOU CAUSE SO MUCH RACKET DURING CLASS!?
Infirmary
I'M SENDING YOU TWO STRAIGHT TO KEENE AFTER THIS!

Look, I was just minding my own business, studying.
WHAT?!
Then **he** comes over and punches me out of nowhere.

Well, Blyke...
None of this would've happened if you hadn't broken my pen!

Augh! Give me a break!
It was the most useless part of the pen!
I don't care! Don't break my stuff!

Shut up.
BAM!

Ouch, that hurts...
It doesn't matter who started the fight.
Understand that your actions have conseq-
Doc...

Help!
SNAP
GONE!
...

Woaba Boba
Of all things, you threw him out of a window?

Well, it's not like I had a choi-

Hey! That's not funny!
So creative...
I could've been killed!

You always say that.

Yet here you are again...
...still in one piece.

You're missing the point.
Come on, it's gotta be at least a little exciting!

Living on the edge seems so fun!

...

Not at all...
I really just want a moment of peace.

Right now, every little conflict always turns into a full-on brawl.
I can't do anything without fearing for my life!
Why does the world have to be so violent?
What's wrong with talking things over with one another?
Because it's a waste of time.
There's no need to argue with a weakling to prove a point...
Because you can just overpower them?
The stronger person isn't always right, you know!
To have to use force to back up your claim... It's so pathetic!
What are you implying?

Sera was born strong.
So she doesn't understand what people like me have to go through every day...

Lovun? That's the next town over!
Could EMBER be heading here?
Puh! X-Static... How useless!

Hm...
...?

And yet another self-proclaimed "superhero"...
...falls victim to the consequences of everyday society...

People need to learn to mind their own business.
Especially if they don't have the strength to back it up.

But he was trying to keep us safe.

SLURP

Do you feel safer...
...now that he's dead?

A year ago, I transferred into Wellston Private High School.

I had worked very hard to get into this school.

Many sleepless nights... Countless hours of studying...
With such difficult entrance exams,
I expected academics to be the main focus at Wellston.

I expected it to be different.

DING
Chatter...

DING
So math is next!

Hi, John!

!!
Welcome to Wellston! I'm Elaine.
How's your first day so far?
SUPER CUTE

Not bad, I guess...
Wonderful! So where did you transfer from?
Erm, actually, I was home-schooled before this!
Whoa, really?
I don't think we've had someone like that before.

Hah...I was feeling a bit lonely, so I decided to try something new!
Well, you've come to the right place!
Great!

But I was wrong...
So, John...
This place was just like the rest of the world.
What kind of ability do you have?

Silence

Well, actually...
...I don't have one.

...

What did you say?

Erm...I don't have an abili–?
I can't believe this!
SNAP
Elaine? Are you all right?
?!
DON'T TOUCH ME!
SHOVE
...
THUMP!
GRRR.

And those without strength are crushed.

Those without strength are nothing.

CHAPTER 2

JOHN'S APARTMENT

RING

RING

RING

RING

RING

HELLO?

Hey, I need to make a trip to the mall today.

Will you come with me?

Ah, sh-shopping?

Sorry, but I'm kinda busy right now...

Oh, really?

Y-yeah, my place is a mess...It'll take all day to clean.

If you'd just move into the dorms like all the other guys...

...this wouldn't be a problem anymore.

Then I'd have to fear for my life.

True.
Hm, that's too bad then...
Yeah, and-!
DING
DING
DONG
DONG
Don't tell me...
Rumble...
Rumble...
Rumble...
WHAM!
YOU'RE ALREADY OUTSIDE?!
GLOOM
...
Aw, don't give me that look.
Come on, I'll help you clean.

SHINY
SHINY

DROP
UNORDINARY
W. H. DOE

There. All done! Let's get going!
...

scratch
Ugh, fine. You got me...
But try to keep it short this time, all right?

KOVORO MALL
ANDY'S
fashion boutique

HEY, SERA!

How's this one?
?!
LA
ME

I think the writing is pretty cool!
"LA ME." It's gotta be French or something.
Wonder what it means...

You're kidding, right?
That says "LAME"...

Fitting Rooms
>

Beep
Beep

He still wanted to try it on...
Beep

...
SHH....
SHAA--
LAME

Good?

Doesn't look half bad...

TAT
TAT
Phew. Didn't expect that to go so smoothly.

Bump!
See? The mall isn't so bad.
Let's not go that far-
ABILITY GAUGE
Measures from 1-10
Score of 5+ gets a prize
$10

ABILITY GAUGE

Measures from 1–10

Score of 5+ gets a prize

GRRR

What do you mean I only got a four?!
SLAM!

But, miss, you should be proud of this score.
You're more talented than the average person!

Bullsh*t! You gave me only a **four**?

Ah, miss. Using the standard gauging system, 2.5 is average and five is considered "high-tier."
So you're very strong. Even I myself would only a two.
You're a fraud!

I want my money back now!
Miss, you can't just–!

Listen to me.
Grab

If you don't refund my money right now, I will blow your entire booth to bits!

Jeez, calm down...

HEY! MIND YOUR OWN BUSINESS, BRAT!

Excuse me? This **is** my business.
I'm not waiting around for your ten-dollar refund.
Stop bullying the guy and give someone else a turn.
CLENCH

HOW DARE YOU SPEAK TO ME THAT WAY!
KIDS LIKE YOU SHOULD KEEP YOUR MOUTHS SHUT!

...

Look, lady! I'm not trying to start a fight!
Let's go somewhere else. This isn't worth the wait.

You should've thought of that before insulting me.

Whoa, now you're just making stuff up.

Okay, I apologize. Let's just talk about this...

Oh? Scared now?

Uh,
yes.

What's in her hand?
Condensed energy...?

A shot of that could do some serious damage...
She did score a four, after all...
SECURITY

Go ahead.
?

If you really want to fight, I'd be happy to oblige.

Why isn't he powering up?

And that girl... She keeps smiling to herself...
DUN...

What are you waiting for?

DON'T BE FRESH WITH ME, BRAT!

SOMEONE HELP!
THIS CRAZY WOMAN'S GOING TO BLOW UP THE MALL!
SECURITY
!!
Miss.
?!
SECURITY
What's going on here?
THEY-!
We were just waiting in line!
Then she suddenly threatened to blow up this booth so we spoke up...
THAT'S BECAUSE HE-!

H-HE SCAMMED ME OUT OF MY MONEY!
...

So it's you again?
I'm getting sick of your bullsh*t!

Return the money that you took from this lady **now**!
But-!

Don't make me repeat myself.
...

I'm warning you...

If you cause trouble one more time...
...I'll make sure you never do business here ever again!

Here you go, miss.

Thank you very much, sir.

bye
Just doing my job.
You two better stay out of trouble!
Leaves
Peek
...
Sorry, we didn't mean to cause you more trouble...
Ah, don't worry about it! I appreciate the gesture.
It doesn't matter where the evidence points...
...the result is always the same.
Speak for yourself...
Not many people are willing to speak up nowadays. So, thank you.

I assume you two are here to have your abilities read?

Yup! She is!
?!
Great! I'll give you a free shot!
It's the least I can do!

...
Incredible! Your ability level is an **eight**!
You're very gifted, miss.
It's been a while since I've met someone as strong as you.
Um... thanks?
Hm...so he gauges abilities through touch.
And...here's your prize!
TAH - DAH!
A cute little bear for a cute little lady!

Hah...It's worth as much as the fee...
...

And what about you, young man? Would you like to try as well?

!!!
AVOID

Oh, sorry.
I should've asked for permission first...

It's no big deal.

STUFF
You wouldn't get anything from me anyway...

Please come back if you ever change your mind!
WAVES
Sure!

OUTSIDE KOVORO MALL
Wow, what a day...
It's already dark out.
That's because you woke up at 2 PM...
Ugh, it's so...
...crowded.
Let's go to a different stop.
There's one across the park.

giggle
What's so funny?
You built that up so much, I thought a war was gonna go down.
But you just ended up screaming for help...
So anticlimactic.
That lady was clearly in the wrong.
But she ended up getting her way just because she was more powerful.
It's so frustrating!
...
Don't be so negative.
Bump!
Worry about yourself more.
At least you didn't break an arm today.
That's true...

Hey, Sera.
...
You come up with a name for this guy yet?
You have something in mind?
How about...
...JOHN.
Wow. Real creative.
What, you don't like it?
!!
...
What is it?

GRAB!
?!
Let's go!
PULL
What's going on?
What are we running from?
This way!
TURN

...
SHUFFLE
THROW
LAND

!!
I-it's invi-
SNAP!

BAM!

BOOM!
-sible!
Let's get outta here.
A-ah, right...!
STOMP!
BACK AT JOHN'S HOUSE

...
PANT
PHEW!

What was that...?
I think some guy was trying to mug us.

Welp, that's enough excitement for today!
stretch

John, how did you know we were being followed?

Ah...
shrug
No idea...

Are you hungry?
I'll make some ramen!

Nah, it's getting late.

I'm going to head back to the dorms.

WHA-?! ARE YOU CRAZY?

You can't go back after that!
What if there are more of them?

I can take care of myself.

I know.
But it's safer if you just stay here!
Why risk it when you can leave once it's bright out tomorrow?

Sigh-
Fine.

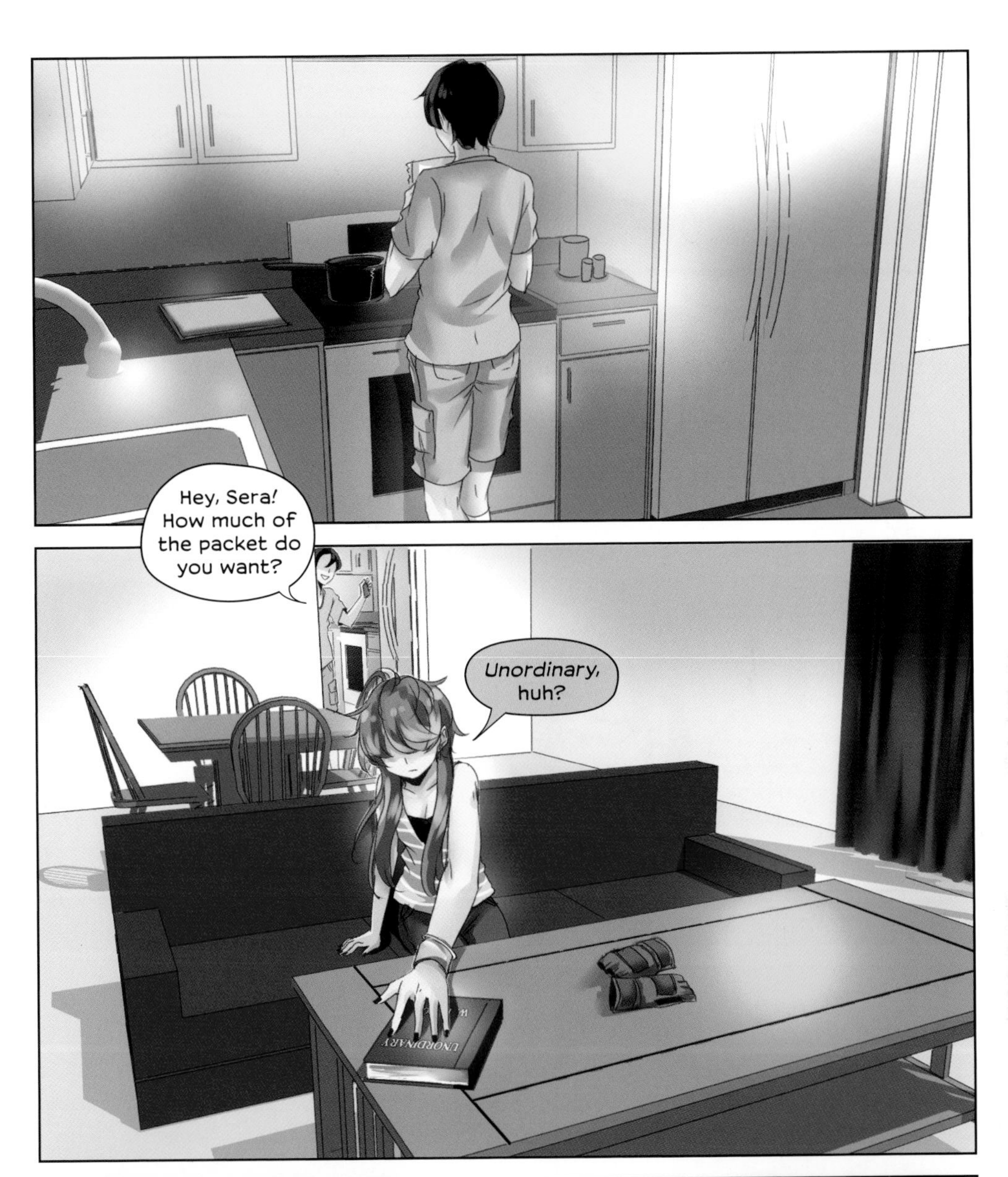
Hey, Sera! How much of the packet do you want?
Unordinary, huh?
UNORDINARY

Crap! I forgot to put that away!

You always surprise me.
UNORDINARY

How'd you get your hands on this?
This book was banned two years ago, almost right after publication!
Is this real?
My dad had a few extras left over, so he gave me one.

Your dad, huh?
AH! YOUR DAD IS THE INFAMOUS W. H. DOE!
Yea...?
UNORDINARY
Infamous?
W. H. DOE

I've always wanted to read this.
But copies are impossible to find.

I wonder how it sparked so much controversy.
...
I didn't know she cared so much...

There are rumors that it's cursed.
...and a lot of people become delusional after reading it.

All these "superheroes" who think they're doing the rest of us a favor...
Like X-Static or whoever else... They've all been influenced.
Isn't it crazy?
They're not delusional.

LATER THAT NIGHT

You really think you can fight back.
We'll teach you a lesson!
Leave me alone!

Stop!

Stop it!

Let me help you.

JOLT
...?!
...
SPLASH
Calm down.

SIGH
It was just a dream...

CONVENIENCE STORE
24/7
tch!
SHFF

click
Well, you're up early.
Couldn't sleep...
Oh, did you have a bad dream?
I got us breakfast!
Come on, let's eat!
Man, I'm starving!
...

He hasn't said a word since he came back...
John.
Is everything all right?

It's nothing.

You know, if something is bothering you-

I told you I'm fine!

...

It seems like...
STAND
...you need some time alone.

I didn't mean to snap!
Ack! Sera, wait!
See you tomorrow.

SIGH

LATER AT WELLSTON DORMITORIES

Were you hanging out with that loser zero again?!

I DON'T GET WHY YOU'RE ALWAYS WITH HIM!
SWOOP!
YOU'RE MAKING YOURSELF LOOK BAD!

And he-!

...!!

Elaine.
Ugh! I can't move!
I've told you...

What I do...
...is none of your business.

DROP

click
...
THUMP!

RING
RING!

RING!

Arlo? Ah, h-hello!
Hey, I'm about to head out.
Is Seraphina there?
Y-yeah, she just got back!
All right, I'm on my way.

...

BZZT!

JOHN
Hey, sorry about earlier..
Be careful with that book, btw. If someone sees it, you might get in trouble
"Be careful with that book, btw. If someone sees it, you might get in trouble."

flip
Dedicated to my son.

KNOCK KNOCK
HIDE

Arlo...
Hey.
Wow, you look beautiful toda-!

NO.

Wait!
At least hear me out.
Go on, then.
We were challenged to a Turf War, and it starts six hours from now...
But we're down a member.
So, I need you to sub in as **Queen**.

...
I'm not interested.

BYE.
PUSH
SERIOUSLY?!

Seraphina, I know it's boring for you...
...but as Wellston's true **Queen**, this is your responsibility!

I've been running the show for you until now...
But today...
...I need a **Queen**.

Where's Remi?
Why isn't she going?

A family emergency.

...
Don't worry,
you won't need to fight those weaklings.
The **Jack** and I will take care of everything.

6 HOURS LATER...

TURF WAR BATTLEGROUND
AGWIN HIGH SCHOOL

WELLSTON HIGH SCHOOL
It's about time!

Broven, it's been a while!
How've you been?

Cut the crap, Arlo!
You're the one who challenged us!
At least have the decency to show up on time!

!!
glare
...
He lied...

My apologies.
So what are you planning?
Wellston has no need to instigate a Turf War.
You're already number one!
walk

I heard you guys just recruited a new **Queen.**
And word is, you haven't lost yet.
I wanted to see her in action.

Be careful what you wish for...
You cocky b*stard!
So how do you want to settle this?
One-on-one or three-on-three?

One-on-one.
Looks like you've changed things up too.
Who's the new girl?
Seraphina.
She's a returning veteran.
Where have I heard that name before?
Wait! **Seraphina?!**
The same one who...
...who instantly took down our entire roster?!

All right, let's get started, then!

Turf War between Wellston and Agwin will now begin.
Jacks, please take your positions!
Whichever team knocks out the opponent's lineup will be victorious!

Power
Defense
Speed
Recovery
Trick
VS.
Power
Defense
Speed
Recovery
Trick
And... **FIGHT!**
DASH

He's fast!
A melee fighter, maybe?

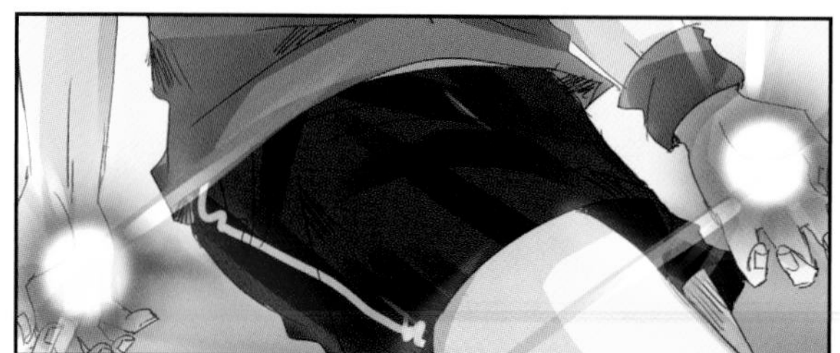

TOSS!!
Don't let him get close!

HWAH!!
Jump!
BOOM!!
What?
He used his
energy beam
to dodge it?

UGH!
JUMP!
How do I get to him?

grab!
THROW

STOP.
YOU'RE FINISHED.
This round's victor is clear! It's our loss.
Healer
I, uh...
It's fine. Come get your leg healed.

Power
Defense
Speed
Recovery
Trick
I will take it from here.
The victor of the previous round was **Jack** from Wellston!
VS.
Agwin's **Queen** has agreed to be the next challenger!
Power
Defense
Speed
Recovery
Trick
BEGIN!

TOSS!
BOOM
?!
BAM!
WHAT THE HELL IS THAT?!
BOOM!

I can't do **anything** with her constantly throwing those things at me!
!!
SPURT!
SLIDE
...
Ugh, great. Of course she goes and spawns two more of them!

BAM!
BAM!
BAM!
BAM!
All right! Now I can get a clean shot on her!

FSHH...

...

WHAMM!!
CRASH!
...
What is he waiting for...?
Augh...
Blyke can't win against her.

DAMN IT!
HOW MANY OF THOSE THINGS DO YOU HAVE?

Still acting tough?
Seriously, why hasn't your team called you back yet?
They're not **really** gonna leave you out to get KO'd, are they?

Shut up!

Fine.
Then I'll end this quickly.
ENOUGH.

There's no point in continuing this match.
Ah...

The win is yours.

Elaine.
A-ah... Yes?
Take care of Blyke.

R-right!

I left Turf Wars for one semester...

...and this is what Arlo made of it?

...

No.
I told you, didn't I?
Blyke and I are going to take care of this.
You **will** sit back and watch.

Nice one!
slap!

Don't let your guard down.

There's a reason why Wellston is ranked first in Turf Wars.
They've never lost a fight before.

Don't worry, Broven.
I won't play around anymore.

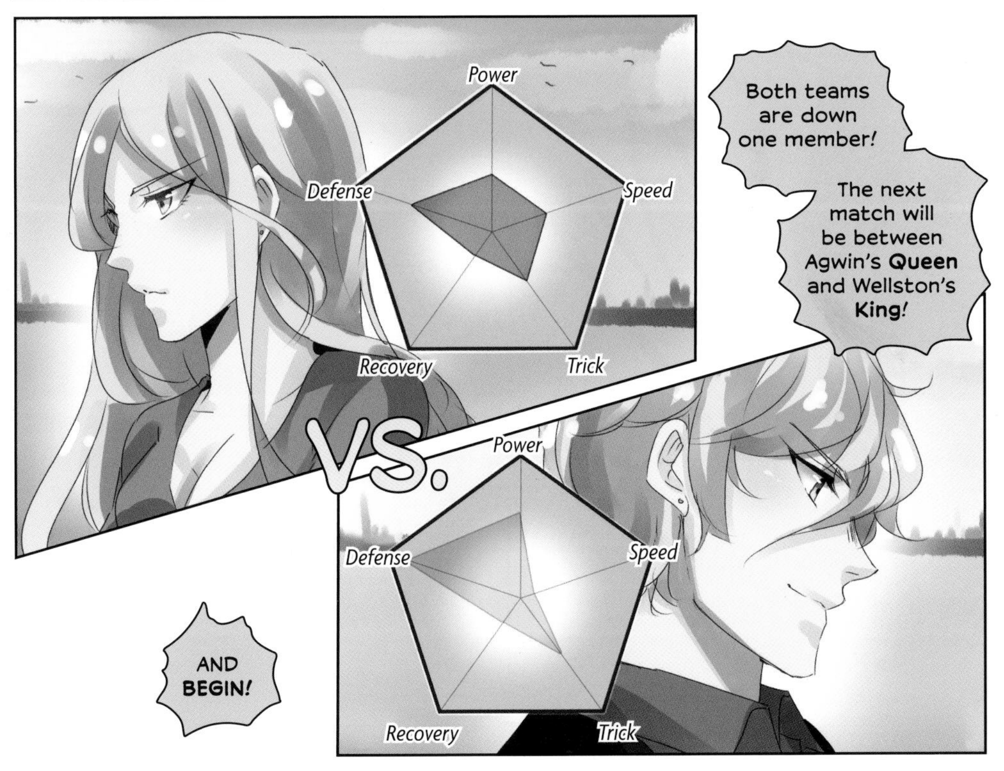
Power
Speed
Trick
Recovery
Defense
Both teams are down one member!
The next match will be between Agwin's **Queen** and Wellston's **King**!
VS.
Power
Speed
Trick
Recovery
Defense
AND **BEGIN!**

BAM!!
A force field, huh?
JUMP

There **must** be a weak point somewhere!
WHAM!
WHAM!
WHAM!
WHAM!
WHAM!
!!

LAND
...
D-DON'T COME ANY CLOSER!
WHACK!
!
BMP!
I'M TRAPPED!
WHAM!
fwp
fwp
BAM!
fwp!

How...?

I thought you
were unbeatable.

step

I SAID
STAY
BACK!

What a
disappointment...

I had heard so
many good things
about you...

But you're
really nothing
out of the
ordinary.
This
prick!

SHUT UP!
miss
Your hits won't do anything.
GRAB
STOP THE FIGHT! WE'VE LOST THIS ONE!
CHOKE!
HEY, ARLO, WHAT ARE YOU PLAYING AT?!
LET HER GO!
THAT'S IT! I'M BREAKING HER OUTTA THERE!

DASH!

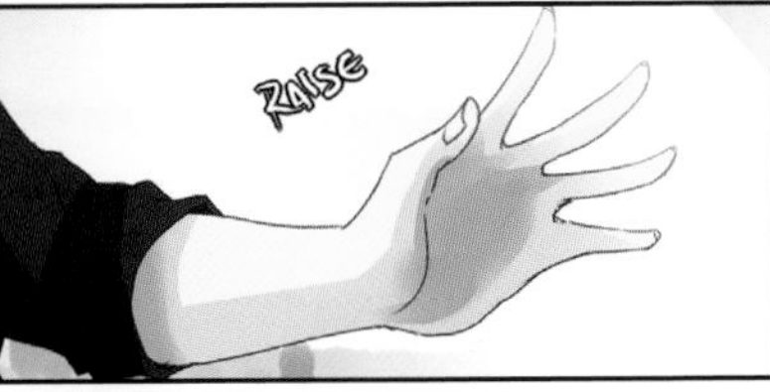
RAISE

BAM!
WAIT, GOU! YOU'RE NOT STRONG ENOUGH TO-!

GUH!

Gou!

Arlo!

That's enough.

Seraphina...

You think after being absent all this time...

...you can just stroll back in and give me orders?

THINK AGAIN.
!!
CHOKE!

WAIT! SERAPHINA!

DON'T!

CRACK!
?!?

CRUNCH!!
Rewind.
GAHH!
SHOVE!
REIN!
DASH!
...
You!

WHAT THE HELL DO YOU THINK YOU'RE DOING?!
YOU WOULD ATTACK YOUR OWN TEAMMATE?!
Well, that's embarrassing.
I've never seen a team fight itself before.
TURN
...
This match is still ongoing.
You have two options.
Either forfeit...
...or continue to fight, with me as your next opponent.
step
step
step
Fine. You win.

...

Elaine.

What happened to Seraphina?

Why did she act up like that?

I don't know...
Nothing I say gets through to her anymore.

What's the point of being her roommate if you can't keep her in check?

It's all because of him...

Seraphina used to be so focused on being the best.
She was always perfect at everything she did, and everyone idolized her.
But ever since she started hanging around that loser, John...
She's become a completely different person.
It's like nothing matters to her anymore.

John?
Ah, that's right! You don't know him...!
You're not in our grade!

He's this guy in our class.
He's a zero

Just the mention of him grosses me out!
They've gotten close lately, and last night...
...she stayed over at his place.

Elaine...
...from now on...
Let me know if she does **anything** suspicious.
As for this John guy...
...I'll deal with him.

Achoo!
!@#!

...
WIPE
Last night, at 8:23 PM...

...authorities discovered a body marked by the infamous EMBER logo.
The body was found in an alley in South Wellston.
The attacks are getting closer...
Like all previous victims, this man's body was covered in burns.
The victim was identified to be ArkRAYgeous, a powerful and popular vigilante.
His death marks the fourth murder that EMBER has committed this month!
So far all EMBER victims are high-tier "superheroes".
Now, let's hear the public's reaction.
DO NOT CROSS.DO NOT CROSS.

Excuse me, sir.
What are your thoughts on the role that vigilantes have played recently?
GGTV

Frankly, I couldn't care less about those lunatics!
They're a bunch of kids just looking for trouble!
GGTV

And what about you, ma'am?
W-well, I find it pretty terrifying...
...hearing about all these powerful people dying.
I mean, I'm grateful for what they have done...
GGTV

...but sometimes, I feel like they bring more trouble than they are worth...
TURN

A lot has been happening lately...and there are things that I'd rather not hear about...
Y-you know what I mean?

WELLSTON PRIVATE HIGH SCHOOL
GoOoOD MORNING!
GAH! SONUVAB*TCH!
PUSH!
CRINKLE

ISEN, WHAT THE HELL IS WRONG WITH YOU?!
YOU'RE SO FREAKING LOUD!
Relax, man.

Whoa, you look terrible.
Did Turf Wars kick your a$$ again?
SHADDAP! AT LEAST I'M STRONG ENOUGH TO MAKE IT ONTO THE ROSTER!
SPIT

Hey, I could too!
I'm just not into that kind of stuff!
Yeahsure whateveryou saybroibelieve you.
Anyway, I'll have you know...
...Seraphina went yesterday.

NO WAY! You got to see her in action?!
Yuuup!
Hehe, that's right!
Aww, man, you are so **lucky!**
She must've wiped the other team out!
Well, actually, she attacked Ar–

Erm...I just remembered, I'm not supposed to talk about it.
Really? You're gonna leave me hanging like that?
...
Come on, I know you can't keep a secret.
Spit it out– you'll feel better.

O-okay, promise you won't tell anyone?
You bet!
PAT
squeeze

I got so carried away with the weekend... Completely forgot I have a huge history test today!
SCRATCH

CRAM
CRAM

BUMP!

Ah, sorry about that.

HEY!
WHAT DO YOU THINK YOU'RE DOING?!

Um... cramming?
GRAB!
YOU JUST BUMPED INTO THE **KING** AND THAT'S ALL YOU HAVE TO SAY?
Look, I said sorry.
What else do you want me to do?
You want an apology too?

If that's all, then can I go?
....
I have a test in 10 minutes.
WHY YOU...!
Is this really necessary?
Calm down.
Uhh...
You're making a big fuss over nothing.
Hey, you said you have a test soon, right?
Uh, yeah.
B-but, Arlo! He-
shove

Good luck, then.
Thanks!
...
TAT
TAT

H-hey...
Wasn't that the guy you were looking for?
Why didn't you take him down?
Did you notice anything off about him?
Yeah! His hair was greasy as hell!
If you had no ability, and you just bumped into the King...
...how would you react?
Er...well, if I were a weakling, I think I'd be careful to not bump into anyone...
B-because I'd be scared of getting beat up...
bump!
That's right.
But not only did he walk straight into me...
...when he turned to apologize...
...I didn't see the slightest hint of fear in his eyes.
Interesting guy...

Beep Beep
PERFECT!

YOUR RATING:
SSS
PERFECT!

....

For as long as I can remember,
I had to be perfect.
"Seraphina, you are not like the others."
"You were born gifted."
"You will rise above your peers."
I must be stronger!
I must be smarter!
I must be perfect!

Before I knew it, I'd become so lost in people's expectations...

Just like how the weak will forever stay at the bottom...

My role was to be at the peak and to be perfect.

So in this school, there's a hierarchy that everyone follows.
And since you're a zero, you're at the very bottom.
You must do **everything** we say.
Hey! Can you help me out here?
That's the **Queen**, you idiot! You can't just talk to her like that!
NEW KID!
PAY ATTENTION WHEN WE SPEAK TO YOU!
whoosh!
WHAM!!
dodge!
FWOOSH!!
Hey, you can't really be thinkin-

...
Two guys against a zero
That's a little overkill...
WHY ARE YOU DOING THIS?!
BLOCK!!
GRAB!
WHAM!

?!
toss!
pull
I HAVE YOUR FRIEND! STOP THE FIGHT!
pissed.

...
Whoa! Nonono–
DASH!
OKAY, FINE! HERE, TAKE HIM BACK!
What am I even watching right now...?
Hey!! Grab that f*cker!
PUSH!
glare...
...
Thanks for nothing.
dash
AFTER HIM!!
This guy...
Who does he think he is?

Seraphina!
Come up and get your test.
Thanks.
Another perfect score, just as expected!
Class, you should all follow Seraphina's example!
Hey, that's not fair, Teach!
She's on a different level than us!
Yeah, everything is too easy for her!
Good grades and strength don't just come from nowhere.
I worked hard to get to where I am.
Hey, I heard we won Turf Wars again!
Well, duh!
We have Seraphina on our team...
TAT
...so we **better** be winning all of them!
Otherwise, I'd be so disappointed in her–ACK!
S-Seraphina!
Hope she didn't hear us!
...

Hey, I got the scoop!
Open
They're serving the Triple Choco Cake today during lunch!
Really? How did you know?!
Hah, don't worry about it
Just make sure you get to the caf early today!
CHOCOLATE CAKE?!
Hehe, I actually got my hands on one!
Can't wait to taste it!
Hey.
What? You again?
I want that cake of yours. Give it to me.

NO WAY.
...
Look, I don't care if you're **Queen**, **King**, **Ace**, or whatever...
...this cake belongs to me!
Go get your own!
...
GLOW
Don't make me repeat myself.
SHIVER

...

OOPS.
DROP!

!
!
!
!
Ohh, what's going on over there?
...
Looks like a standoff between Seraphina and the zero!

You're nothing.

You're so far below me!

YOU DON'T GET TO STAND UP TO ME!

SMACK!
YOU THINK YOU'RE TOUGH BECAUSE OF WHAT YOU JUST DID?!
WHO THE HELL ARE YOU?!
HOW DARE YOU!?
I WORK SO HARD EVERY SINGLE DAY!
YOU THINK YOU CAN JUST WALTZ IN AND HUMILIATE ME LIKE THIS?!
YOU DON'T EVEN KNOW WHAT'S GOING ON!
SMACK!
What's gotten into her?!
Ugh, I'm getting out of here before she starts targeting me!
SMACK!
YOU'RE SO WEAK AND SO IGNORANT!
SMACK!!
She's snapped!
YET YOU WALK AROUND LIKE YOU OWN THE PLACE!
SMACK!!
SMACK!
LIKE YOU CAN DO WHATEVER!

I made it...I'm at the top!
So why do I still have to follow the rules?

Why do I have to impress everyone?
Why don't I get to do what I want?

beep!
JOHN

Definitely failed that history test...
beep!
Wanna get some lunch?

So apparently, Seraphina beat up Arlo at Turf Wars yesterday!
What? But that's friendly fire! She can't do that!
Yeah, she's been breaking a lot of rules lately. What's wrong with her?

She doesn't go to class anymore, and she chopped off all her hair! Plus she–

whisper
whisper
whisper
whisper

WELLSTON DORMITORIES

Fwp
UNORDINARY
W. H. DO

Dedicated to my son.

CLOSE
UNORDINARY

I need some fresh air...
Toss

Hey, Seraphina!
My parents sent some oranges from home!

They make for great orange juice!
Want some?

Yeah. Later.
O-okay!
I-I'll make some for you, then!

A story about one man who defends a world of zeros?
TAT
TAT
...
How strange...

Where did this premise even come from?
TAT

The idea of a more just society. One with a lot less violence, and a lot less danger...
...so that John can stand as everyone's equal.
Many people seem to actually **agree** with this idea...

And they've taken matters into their own hands, declaring themselves "superheroes"...

...and helping others.

Just like how the protagonist of Unordinary protected zeros.

It's no wonder the authorities banned this book...

...because it challenges the entire structure of our current society.

The fact that some high-tiers even acted on it...

Must've been frightening for them.

Despite everything, there is one glaring similarity between the Unordinary *world and ours...*

Only the powerful are able to influence the outcome of something. They decide whether to use their ability for others...

or to keep it for themselves

OPEN

TAP

Hi Seraphina!
Hope you like this fresh-squeezed orange juice

CLAP!
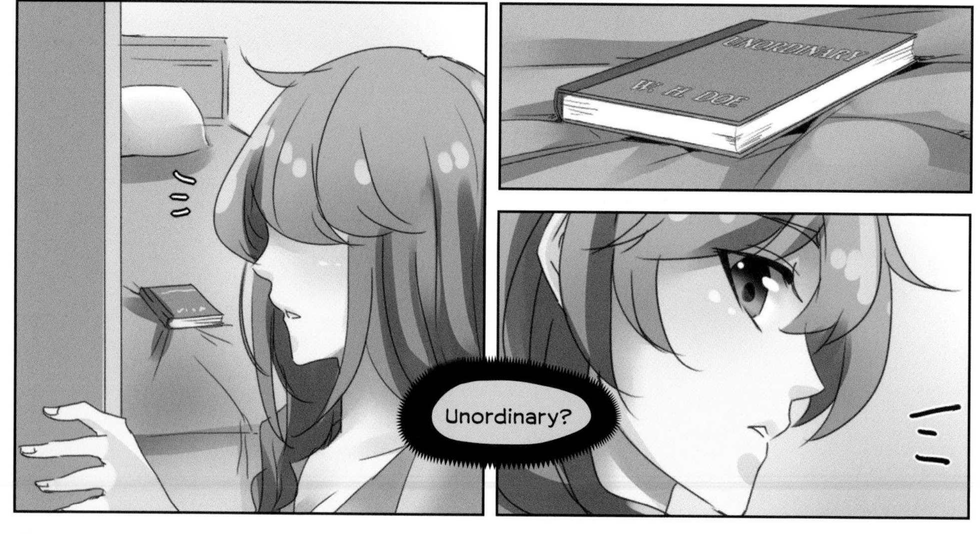
UNORDINARY
W. H. DOE
Unordinary?

"*Unordinary*" is a novel written by author W. H. Doe. It w
banned a few months after publication because it was s
have caused an influx of vigilante. Content of this novel i

/ˌvijəˈlan(t)ē/
noun: vigilante; plural noun: vigilantes

a member of a self-appointed group of citizens who undertake law
enforcement in their community without legal authority, typically
because the legal agencies are thought to be inadequate.

Other: *"Superheroes" or "Super-vigilante" are high-tier vigilantes - those with ability level of 5.0 or higher.*

RECENT NEWS: Several "Superheroes" have been murdered in the last month by the infamous gang EM

SHAKE

Hi, Arlo!
U-um... I think Seraphina is in trouble!

I found this book called *Unordinary* in her room...
...and it looks like bad news!

Elaine.
Does anyone else know?
Um...n-no.
All right, keep it that way.
O-okay!

OPEN

Dang.

JOHN'S HOUSE
Dad
RING
RING

RING
RING

Dad?
Hey, John!
Everything going all right over there?
Yeah, same as usual.
Why? Did something happen?

Well, I'm sure you've already heard...EMBER's causing trouble around your area.
Make sure you stay safe, all right?!
I know, Dad!
You don't need to yell. I'm right here...

John. I mean it. Don't do anything stupid.
Oh, and–AH CRAP!

My editor is calling me!
Anyway, take care of yourself, okay, son?
Yeah, you too, make sure you eat!
Bye.
click

What happened to **you**?
I just found out report cards come out this Friday...

MAN, even the thought of it makes me anxious!
SIGH

Easy for you to say! They're not your grades!
There's nothing you can do about it now, so there's really no point in freaking out.

Hey, John...
I don't think I can give that book back to you.

...

Elaine found it, didn't she?
Well...
AW COME ON, SERA!
I even warned you and every-thing!
beep beep
Game over
You might have godly abilities, but you can't rewind all your mistakes!
OKAY. I GET IT. I MESSED UP.

So, Sera, what did you think of the book?

I figured I wasn't getting the full picture...
...so maybe you can explain it to me.
Well...
I really admired the hero of *Unordinary*...
Because he was the most powerful, yet he realized that everyone has something valuable to offer.
SHT
Same goes for our world, the weakest people can have the greatest ideas.
That's why I'm thankful for all the vigilantes out there who are making this a reality.
If I were qualified, I'd join them 100 percent!
John...
I'm sorry.
I know that book meant a lot to you.
Ah, that's okay!
I've read it plenty of times already.
It's about time I took a break from it...

WELLSTON LIBRARY
I don't get why teachers always like to give tests at the end of the quarter...

THUMP

Now I have a million exams to make up!
Remi!
When did you get back?
Last night.
CLOSE

All right, Blyke, fill me in. What did I miss last week?

Nothing much. We won Turf Wars against Agwin on Sunday.
Seraphina substituted for you as **Queen**.

Wait, also...
lean
This is a secret only **Royals** can know about...
Seraphina kicked Arlo's a$$!

Remi...?

I...I went home to attend a funeral...

...my brother was murdered.

HOMEROOM

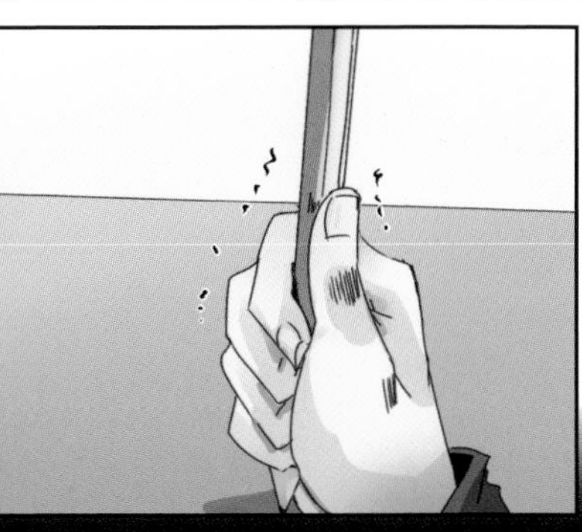

HA HA HA HA

...
..just a bunch of lowlifes!
GRIND..

John, are you okay?

Here, let me help you!

Class, I'll be handing your report cards out now!

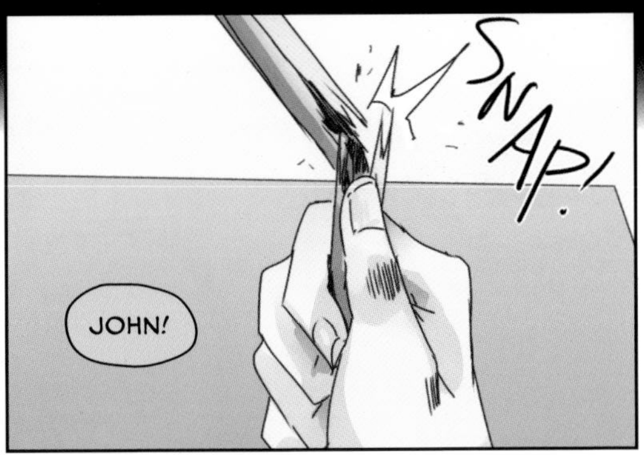
SNAP!
JOHN!

!!
Quickly! Before I start reading your grades out loud!

Ah, right!

...

Eh... it could be worse...

Seraphina always gets what she wants...
So it's no surprise she managed to find a copy of that book.

But I wonder if Unordinary is the reason why...
TAT
TAT

...she would rather associate herself with a zero instead of hang around other high-tiers.
Could she be acting impulsively because of the book's influence?
BUMP!!
OOF!!
Of **course** I bump into this guy...

Oh, it's **you** again?
Is this guy's jaw made of steel or something?
Hey, have you ever heard of a binder?

Uh, yeah. Sorry...
I just got my grades back and was reading the teacher's comments.

...
COURSE
GRADE
TEACHER'S COMMENTS
History C-
Trigonometry B-
Chemistry C+
English C
Language C-
Phys. Ed B-

whisper
whisper
What's happening?
Arlo just kneeled in front of the zero?

SNAP
Don't you all have better things to do?
ACK!

Here.
Ah, thanks.
Report card

Don't mention it.
Next time, watch where you're walking.

WELLSTON CLASSROOM
Uh...
So, you called for me...?
Isen, I need your expertise.
You can find any information on anyone, right?
Well, that's kind of an overstatement...
But what are you looking for specifically?
Do you know that guy in your grade, John?
The zero who always hangs around Seraphina?
Yeah, he's pretty infamous. Why?
I had a few encounters with him...
...and he seems suspicious.
He's powerless and completely unaware of his surroundings...

...gets mediocre grades...
And he has no respect for the social hierarchy.
Someone as useless as him should've been put in his place ages ago.
Yet somehow, he got into one of the top schools...

So I want you to look into it.
Find out what he's hiding...
What his history is...
How he got accepted into Wellston...
Everything.

That seems excessive.
He probably just got lucky-
glow
Isen.
I don't remember asking for your opinion.

shudder
Ah, my bad.
Okay, then, just leave it to me.

Oh, one more thing.

Keep your mouth shut this time.

Death POOL

Which superhero will die next?
PLACE YOUR BETS NOW!

1. GENIE ||||
2. HURRICANE 卌
3. SHATTERSTACK 卌 卌 ||
4. MISTRESS EMERALD |||
5. GALAXY-GAL 卌 |
6. VENOM ||

DEAD LIST
Radiance
Equinox
X-Static
ArkRAYgeous

Who the hell...

Which superhero will die
PLACE YOUR BETS NOW!
1. GENIE
2. HURRICANE
3. SHATTERSTACK
TRESS EMERALD
GALAXY-GAL
6. VENOM
DEAD LIST
Radiance
Equinox
X-Static
ArkRAYgeous
...would do something like this?

CRINKLE
Playing games with people's lives... Disgusting!

NOOO! PLEASE STOP IT!
STOMP!
STOMP!
That'll teach you to walk into me, you little runt!
I STAYED UP ALL NIGHT TO FINISH THIS PROJECT!

Heh, well that's just too ba-

BAM!!

DASH

You think this is funny?
GUH!
There are people dying out there, trying to save your a$$.
TUG

And here you are wrecking other people's projects!
How pathetic.
You're a disgrace to society!

You-
Haha...
Yeah, like you're one to talk.

STUPID ZERO! I'M GONNA BLOW YOUR FACE OFF!

CRACK!
PUSH

Whu-?

SMASH!
BUMP!
SHUT THE F*CK UP!

What the...?!

I WASN'T DONE TALKING YET!

FLINCH!
...

!!

Relax

confused
Huh?

DASH
Yeah, you **better** run away, idiot!

Death POOL
Which superhero will die next?
PLACE YOUR BETS NOW!
1. GENIE
2. HURRICANE
3. SHATTERSTACK
4. MISTRESS EMERALD
5. GALAXY-GAL
6. VENOM
DRIP
DRIP
DEAD LIST
Radiance
Equinox
X-Static
ArkRAYgeous
X-Static

WELLSTON GIRLS' DORMITORIES

KNOCK
It's Remi.
Come in.

...?

There's something inside...?

What is it?
Uh...
I know how much you hate Turf Wars and working with Arlo...
...and I really appreciate you subbing in for me!
BOW
Thank you, Seraphina.
You don't need to thank me.
I owed it to you.
All this time, you've taken the **Queen's** burden off my shoulders.
It's the least I could do.

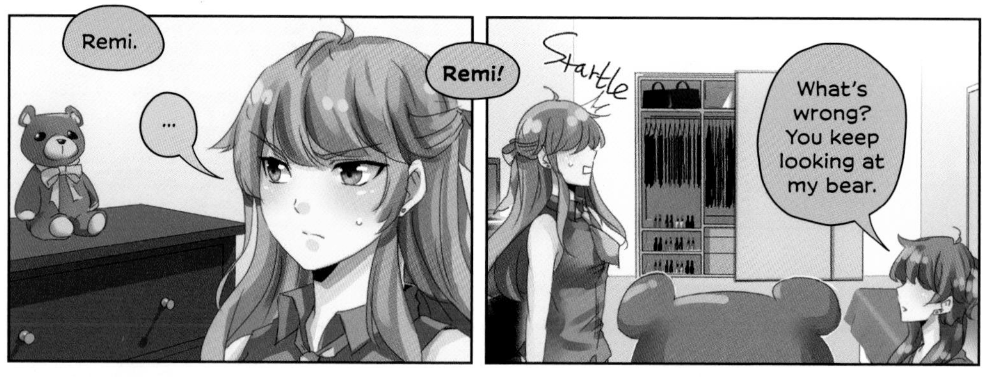
Remi.
...
Remi!
Startle
What's wrong? You keep looking at my bear.

Ah, there's a circuit inside...
It's throwing me off a bit.
What?

So you didn't know?
GRAB

In that case...
Mind if I take a look?
Hm...all right.

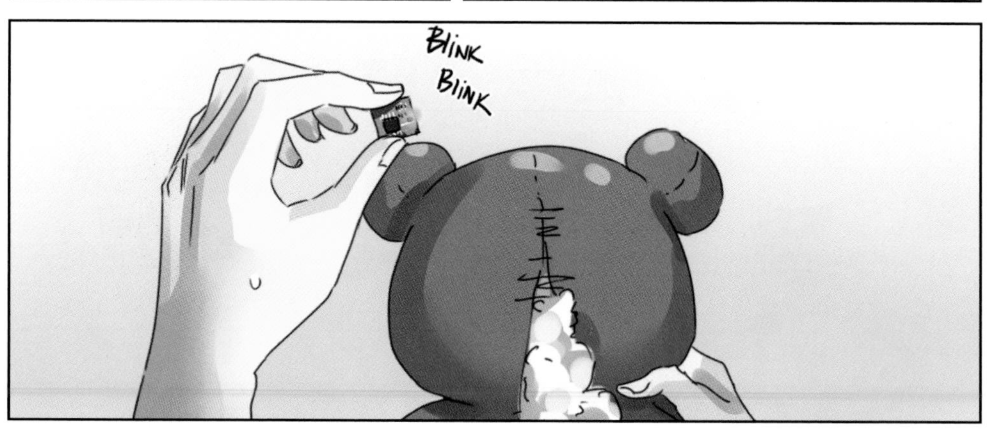
BLINK
BLINK

!!
ZZZAP!
It's some kind of transmitter.
Looks like someone's been tracking you...
The man at the mall...
Did he plant a tracker in all of the prizes?
Could he be targeting high-tiers?
You should stay alert from now on.
We may be strong... but we're far from invincible.
Seraphina...

What the hell...?

Of all the information I've gathered so far...

John? He plays dirty!
Bluffed me out and threw me out a window...
Then he got Seraphina to kick my a$$.
He doesn't even fight his own battles.
Uhhh...we fought him a looong time ago.
Pls dun hurt us!
I can't really remember...
He definitely ended up running away, though. Too scared to face us.

JOHN? WHO THE F*CK IS THAT?
RAGE
A-ah, sorry to bother you!

Nothing out of the ordinary...
John acts exactly how a zero should.
BITE

AUGH! Stupid Arlo!
Making me look for something that doesn't even exist!
ALSJLKSDJF WHY ME!?

If I don't report to him soon, he'll have my hea–!
Wait.

Bluffing his way out?
CRACK!
Not fighting his own battles?
SMASH!
BUMP!
Running away scared?
DASH
That's not what I saw.
He knew exactly what he was doing!

John!

Hi
Isen?

You talking to me?
You're John, aren't you?

The Press Club wants to write an article about low-tiers.
So I need to ask you a few questions.
Sure! I'd be happy to help!
But can it wait till later? My class is about to start.

Haha, that's a good one.
PAT
But I wasn't kidding...

No, it can't.

Glad you could make it, John.
Please, have a seat.
broken

I didn't get much of a choice...
You practically dragged me here...
I've always wanted to say that! :D

Yeah, whatever... Sit down, will ya?
shuffle

Remember, I'm doing this to shed light on low-tiers.
So give me your full **honesty**.

That's... really generous of you.

So John...
...where are you from?
twirl
New Bostin.
Now...
...let's find out what you're hiding.

Whoa! That's pretty far from here!
Is that where you went before Wellston?
WAVE
No no!
I've been homeschooled for my entire life. This is the first **real** school I've attended.

Oh right. You mentioned that when you first transferred in.
Yup!

So what made you decide to switch?

I've always wanted to see what a real school was like.
It's just my dad was a bit protective of me, so I didn't get a chance to till recently.

Okay! And how has your experience here been so far?

Uh...

Pretty awful, to say the least...

Could you elaborate on that? It's for the article.
Well...

We're not able to defend ourselves, so everywhere is a danger zone for us.
And because we're so weak...
...it's hard for us to do or say what we want.

One unlucky run-in could put us out for weeks!
Sounds rough.
Scribble

Whoa, he's taking a lot of notes!

So...
...what do you do to survive this lifestyle?
Well, we usually–
NO.

I meant **you** specifically.
Um...I try not to draw any attention to myself.
Just walk along the edge of the halls and stay quiet, you know?

Lies.
If I could include one thing in this article, I'd say...
...we should all accept each other's differences, because–

Hold on. Let's not get ahead of ourselves...
I'm not done asking questions yet.

Why did you pick Wellston as your final choice?

I wanted to go to a top school...
It's got one of the best academic programs in the nation.

HOW AMBITIOUS!

...
Why did he suddenly become so aggressive?

But...
...you must've known that Wellston is one of the most powerful schools in terms of ability level.

It's risky for a zero like you to come here, yet you still did?

Ah...I assumed academics would take precedent over fighting.
What about your father, though? You said he was protective of you.
Surely he had a say too! He didn't warn you about what would happen?
Where's he going with this...?
Clench

See, if it were me...
I'd have enrolled you into a school closer to home for a trial run first!

Unless, that **is** what he did.
And for some reason, things didn't work out over there...

So then you decid-
SLAM!

ISEN!

WHAT KIND OF BULLSH*T ARE YOU PULLING?!

I came here to talk about the struggles of a low-tier.
Not to have you meddle in my life.

You are **so** lucky Seraphina has your back.
GRAB
FLINCH
Get your hand off me.
SQUEEZE
UGH!
THROB
Well, thanks for the input.
PICK UP
You should probably get back to class.

...
New Bostin, huh?

LIBRARY
click
click
NEW BOSTIN HIGH SC
Class 2-B of 201X
!!
I FINALLY FOUND YOU!
STAND
!!
What the-?
Isen, will you **shut up**?
You're gonna get us kicked out of the library again!
flop
Yeah, whatever.
quiet
squint
Hey, man, take a look at this!
Uhh...
What am I even looking at?
You stalking girls from other schools again?
Dude, we have an essay due tomorrow.

No, you idiot!
Are you blind? I'm pointing at the guy!
So you're going for guys too now?
That's John, from two years ago!
And...why are you looking him up?
U-um...

Tell and you die.
Fork
Actually, that's none of your business.
Huh? What the hell's wrong with you?
You called me over first!

Hey, don't you have an essay to write or something?
Get back to work.
SKOOT
F*cking weirdo.

YOU TWO AGAIN?!

UH-OH.
BUSTED.

LATER THAT AFTERNOON

PASS
So I looked into his hometown...
And check out what I found!

That's a class photo of John from his previous school.
He went there for about two years before transferring to Wellston.

That's John?
I hardly recognized him.

Looks authoritative, doesn't he?

Now with this in mind, let's reassess his behavior.
He doesn't care where he walks.
He speaks casually to high-tiers without a second thought.
And he starts fights with whomever he wants.

If it weren't for the fact that he claims he's a zero...
...I'd undoubtedly assume he has an ability. Don't you agree?
Arlo, if you give me a bit longer, I can find out everything-
Tear

Oh sh*t, what now?

You've done enough, Isen.
I'll take it from here.

WELLSTON DORMITORIES
Beep!

New message
from Arlo!

ARLO
Hi Arlo, would you like some oranges?
Sent 1 week ago
Elaine, you should inform the headmaster about what you found the other day.

...
DROP

SERAPHINA, PLEASE REPORT TO THE MAIN OFFICE.

OPEN

TAT
TAT

GLARE

GRAB

FIX

Seraphina. There you are!
Please sit.

Headmaster.
nod

Oh, don't look so tense! You're even making me nervous!

Allow me to introduce you!

This is Miss Nadia. She's here on behalf of the authorities today.
She is going to ask you a series of questions.

Don't worry, you'll be out of here in no time.

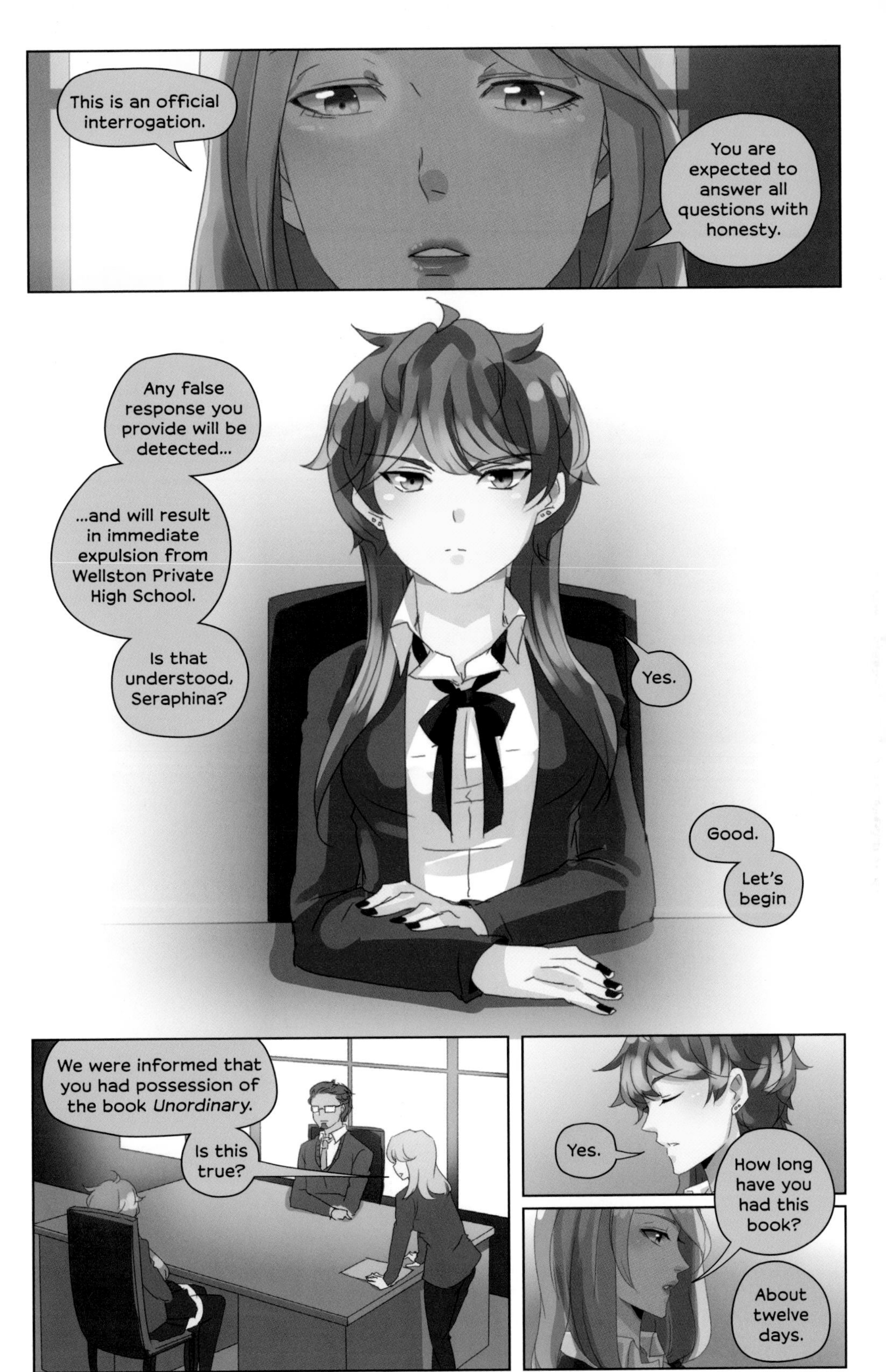
This is an official interrogation.
You are expected to answer all questions with honesty.
Any false response you provide will be detected...
...and will result in immediate expulsion from Wellston Private High School.
Is that understood, Seraphina?
Yes.
Good.
Let's begin
We were informed that you had possession of the book *Unordinary*.
Is this true?
Yes.
How long have you had this book?
About twelve days.

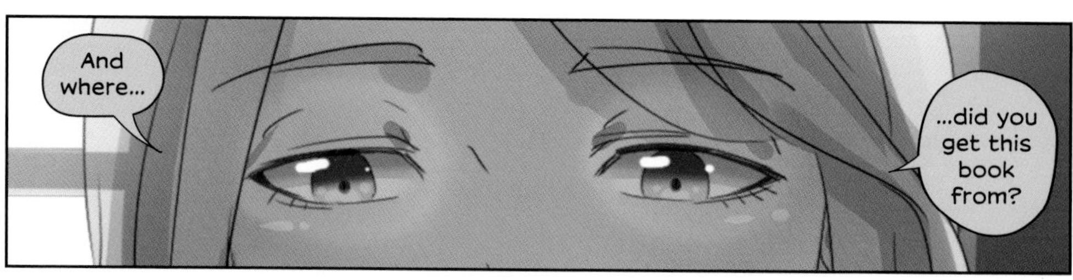
And where...
...did you get this book from?

...

Clench

I can't involve John.

If this woman was sent here as an interrogator...
then her ability could be anything from Mind-Reading to simple Lie Detection.
And judging from her expression, it doesn't seem like she knows what I'm thinking.
Answer the question!

Last Saturday, on my way home from Kovoro Mall, I was followed by an invisible entity.
I fought it off, then ran.
When I got back to the dorms, the book was already in one of my bags.
GLINT
This girl...is not lying.
Where and when did this incident take place?
The bus stop near the park, around 8 PM.
Who else was with you at the time?

Ugh! Seriously?
SNAP

Now, now, Miss Nadia...
My students are all very busy.

Please respect their time by asking questions that are relevant.

Ah, yes. I'll be brief.
Where is the book now?
I destroyed it.
Did you read it while it was in your possession?
I did.

And did you share the book or its contents with anyone?
I did not.
Final question.
What are your thoughts on the content of *Unordinary*?

Honestly, I thought it was a bit absurd.
That's it, I'm going back to class!
I thought the idea was absurd.

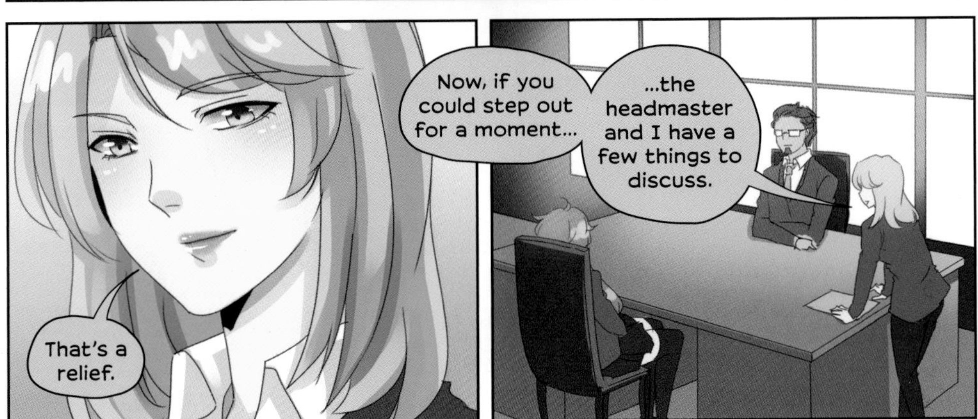
That's a relief.
Now, if you could step out for a moment...
...the headmaster and I have a few things to discuss.

BZZT.
SERA
232! Suck it!
304.
Sent 2 hours ago
Meet me by the school gates ASAP.

Sera!

What's the luggage for?
I have a flight home in two hours.

Elaine ratted me out after all.

And they decided to suspend me for a month..
WHAT?! THAT'S INSANE!

With all the high-tiers dying lately...
...the authorities want to make sure I don't spread the book's ideas around.

At least they won't be coming after you anytime soon.
I managed to trick the lie detector!

It was pretty difficult.
And I almost got caught twice.
Good thing the headmaster stepped in!
Hahaha

GRAB
Sera!

This isn't a joke!
What if you had been found out?
Then neither your reputation nor the headmaster could have saved you!
You should've just told the truth!

The book was mine...
...All this started because of me.
It's fine.
Point is both of us got through this relatively unscathed.

When I'm back next month, this'll all be behind us.

And we'll never have to hear about *Unordinary* again.
I guess that's true.

HONK!!

Oh, that's probably my cue to go...

I'll text you when I get home.
WAVE

WAVE

TAT
TAT

GLOOM-

Hey, Arlo.

What do we do now that Seraphina is gone?

Nothing.

What?

We wait for news to spread.

And watch the school break him down...
TAT
TAT
TAT
Bit by bit.

Hey you!
Crap.
That sounds like...

Long time no see.
I believe we still have some unfinished business.
CRACK—

No, you have the wrong guy. BYE!
HEY!

Get back here, you little b*tch!

Still caught up on the whole window thing?
Look, man! Keep dwelling on the past, and you won't move forward!
DASH

STOP!!
Dead end?!

KICK!!
I've got you now!

SLIDE
LOCK!
!!
PUSH
TRIP!
GAH!
BAM!
WHAM!

Why you little–!
HUH?!

You'll pay for that!

Where...?

In his empowered form, he's much faster than me!
If he catches up, then I'm screwed!
If I can just get around that corner, then–!
TACKLE!!
DAMN IT! TOO SLOW!

THUD
A zero like you thinks he can outrun **me**?!
So heavy...

I won't fall for your stupid tricks again.

PRESS
Nobody's here to save you!

IT'S PAYBACK TIME!

WHAM!!

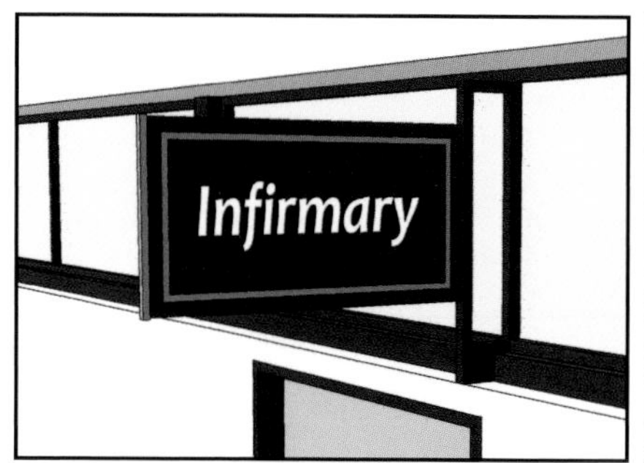
Infirmary

Back so soon?

It hasn't even been four hours since Seraphina left...
...and you already got into a fight.
Why are you smiling though? It's creeping me out...

Keene and I...
We made a bet to see how long it would take you to break something after news of Sera's suspension got around.
Now he owes me fifty bucks.
SPURT
WHAT THE HELL, DOC?

So, just for today...
...I won't give you a hard time.
If you had come in any later...
...I would've strangled you.
Gee, thanks.

...

BUZZ...
BUZZ...

STARTLE
!!!

SERA
Meet me by the school gates ASAP.
Sent 4 hours ago
Just got off the plane.

Beep
Beep

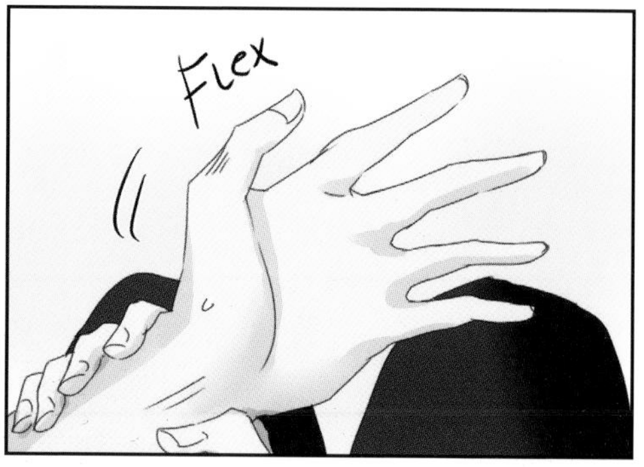
Flex

Impressed

Looks like it's just about healed.
So fast! Doc, your tonics are getting better!

Well, funny you mention that...

Huh?
THANKS TO A CERTAIN SOMEONE, I GET TO PRACTICE MAKING THEM...

EVERY.
SINGLE.
DAY.

RING RING

chatter...
Yo, John!

SLAM!
That's a good look for you.
Uh, can I help you?

Word around school is...
...Seraphina's been suspended.
Not this again...

So the girls and I wanted to borrow you for some target practice after classes today.

So how 'bout it?
You pricks...

What a waste of time.
You three weaklings wouldn't be able...

...to land a single hit on me.

YOU BETTER WATCH WHAT YOU SAY, PUNK!
Huh?
GRAB

!!
I WANT EVERYONE HERE TO KNOW THAT I HAVE A DATE TONIGHT.
AND IF ANYONE MAKES ME WORK OVERTIME...

...I'LL KILL THEM. GOT IT?

I'll be watching!
Y-YES SIR!
STOMP!

Lucky you!

But remember this...

Someone like you will never be more than a leech who feeds off others.

"A leech who feeds off others."

SERAPHINA'S HOME

click
Mom, I'm home.

Seraphina.

SLAP!
You're becoming more and more reckless.

At this rate, you'll end up a failure just like your sister.

Clop.
I want to see those ridiculous extensions gone by the time your father and I return.
We'll discuss your punishment then as well.
Clop
Clop.

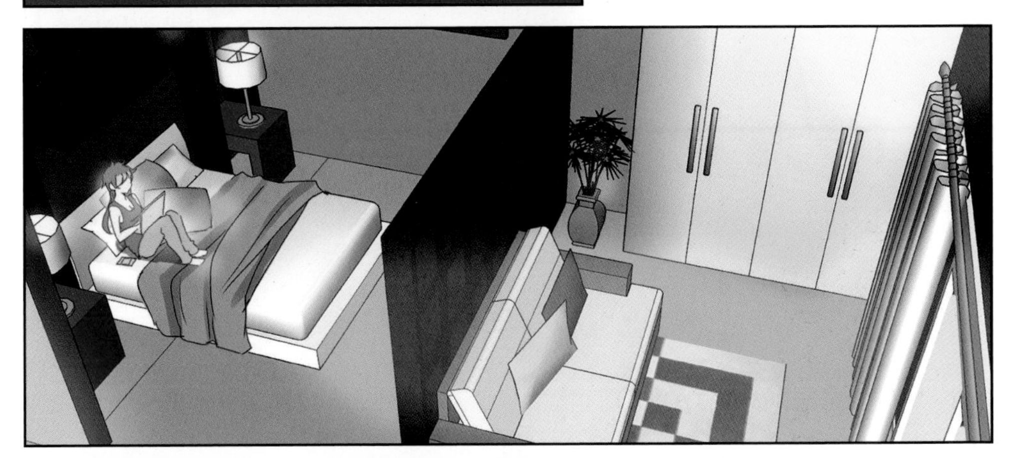

New
Message!
beep

JOHN
Just got back from workout. You have time to talk?

Beep

Ring
Ring
Hey.

Ah...

H-hi!
Pretty awkward greeting...
For someone who was texting so diligently earlier...
Your voice surprised me, that's all.
Feels like I haven't heard it in forever.
Miss me already?

Yeah, I...
...had a long day.

SMACK!!
I spent the last two periods in the infirmary!
Totally forgot to grab the homework from the teachers!
I can't afford to miss any more assignments!
AW MAN!!
Oh. They email the assignments to me every day.
SERA in-call for 03:23:42
I'll forward them to you.
Nice. Thanks.
Yeah, I took a look at it earlier.
It's pretty easy.
Hah...you and I have different definitions for "easy."
Okay, sent.
GOT IT!
So, Sera.
Hm?
How's home?
Must be nice to be with your family again.

My parents just left for a business trip.
So no one's around except for the servants.

OH, I found a new game today! Hurry up and finish so we can play together!
UH...
I'm trying!

Geez! I can't keep up with you!
I only just got the hang of SlappyPig...
Don't worry, this one's easier.
It's called AngryPigs.
More pigs?
level 51 17831
The title doesn't make much sense...
...because you play as a family of happy birds.
But the point is to build houses and protect them from airborne attacks...
From falling angry pigs that explode.
Boom!
Boom!
HUH? That escalated quickly!
Yup, and if you have a single bird alive after the attack...
...then you move on to the next level.
It's really fun, I promise.
Sounds pretty complicated...
Okay, okay. Lemme finish up, and I'll play a round.

Level 13
1973
YOU LOSE!
John.
SERA
in-call
for
07:35:56
This is bullsh*t.
If you want to stop sucking at this game...
...then you need to start building your houses with glass.

But that doesn't even make sense!
Plus it costs too much!
Who's ever heard of glass being stronger than wood?!

That's just what the developers decided. Deal with it.

NO!
You just watch!
Click
I'll beat this level without using any glass!
Click
Hm. Good luck with that...

Oh, but you might wanna do that some other time...
Huh, why?
It's almost 2 AM.
WHAT?!

TAT
TAT

SERA
Just woke up. Good thing no school today :p
So what? You don't go to class either way.

You.

GRAB

I told you to watch where you walk.

Uh...
sorry.

...
Will you let go of me plz...?
SERA

He doesn't seem affected by all these recent events.

SERA
Just woke up. Good thing no school today :p

Tch!

?!

Can't have you talking to **her**.
TAT
TAT

That phone needs to go.

LATER THAT DAY
AUGH!

That's it?
Well, what'd you expect? He's a zero, after all.

I mean, he didn't even fight back...

...
Whatever, we're done here.
Let's go.

INFIRMARY
Two broken ribs and a dislocated shoulder!
Not to mention a ton of other minor injuries...

You really outdid yourself this time, John!
Look, Doc!

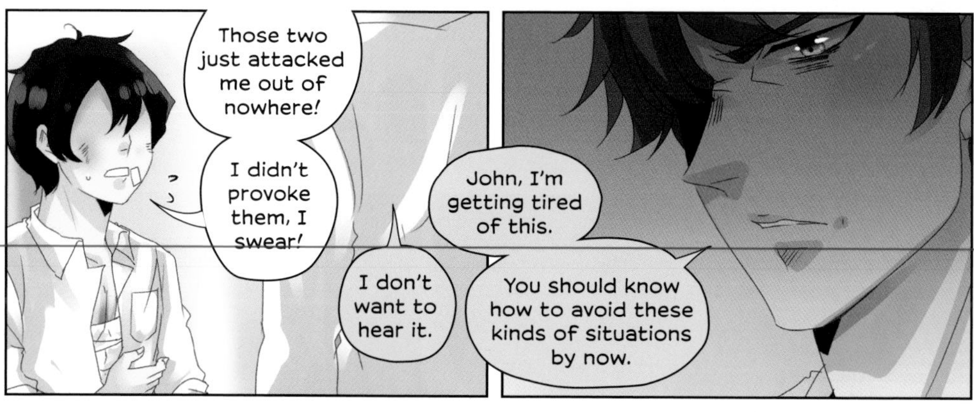
Those two just attacked me out of nowhere!
I didn't provoke them, I swear!
I don't want to hear it.
John, I'm getting tired of this.
You should know how to avoid these kinds of situations by now.

TAT TAT

Oh, that's right...
I haven't texted Sera back yet!
REACH

?!

Hi, Leilah.
I had a great time last night.
I'd like to take you out again sometime.
Oh, Saturday?
Sure, I'll be free then.
Sounds great. I'll pick you up!
SMASH!!!
SLAM!!
WHAT NOW?!
Those two!

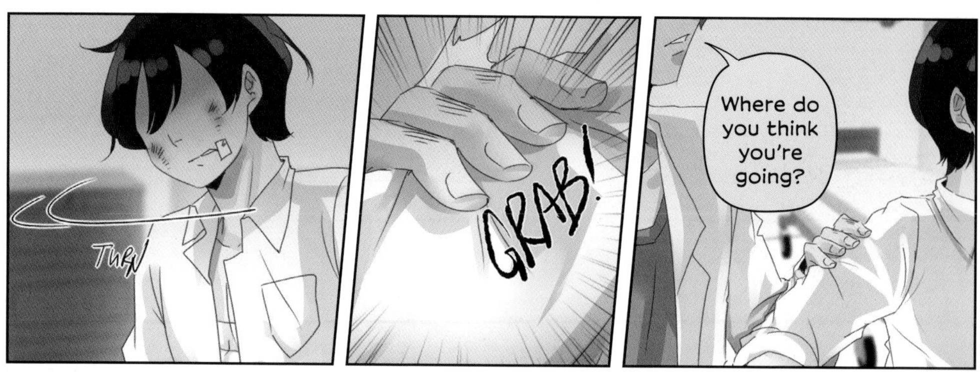
TURN
GRAB!
Where do you think you're going?

SHOVE
?!
LET GO!

You little...

Doc.
I didn't come to school so I could spend all day in the infirmary.

I'm leaving.

DON'T...
...take another step!
Just what the hell do you expect to accomplish by going out looking like that?
You'll have an even **bigger** target on your back!
Honestly, Doc.
I'm not the one you should be worrying about.
My policy exists to **reduce** student injuries.
If you leave now... regardless of what happens, you'll only cause me more trouble.
So, if you have **any** respect for me, you'll sit back **down**!

Fine.
BUMP!

John...

Why are you doing this to yourself?

HEY, ZERO! GET OUT OF THE WAY!
SHOVE!
?!

SCATTER

Haha, that was hilarious!
Hmph, serves him right!

Ew, he's so gross.
Yeah, what a total loser, amirite?

Isn't that Seraphina's friend?

He looks pretty roughed up.

Hey, are you okay?

Here...

Let me help you!

SLAP!!
GET AWAY FROM ME YOU B*TCH!

HUFF
HUFF
HUFF
HUFF

?!

!!

...
THROB
Uh,
I-I'm...
Sorry-
FWOOSH
CLANG!
SHH-

Give me one reason why I shouldn't kick your a$$ right now!
I-I mistook her for someone else...

What kind of excuse is that?

Blyke!
It's fine, just let it go.
...
TUG

"I really admired the hero of Unordinary*... He realized that everyone has something valuable to offer."*

You didn't text back today...

Yeah, I got into a fight and my phone broke.

Ah, well, that's a bummer.
Should've been able to tell by your hair...

It's not like him to be upset for so long...

Hey, don't let it get you down.
Phones are replaceable.
I guess.

Let's talk about something else.
Did you get any further in AngryPigs?
Yes, actually!
Last night I managed to beat a few more levels!!
With 100% wood!
I'm gonna see just how far I can get like this.

PFFTT-
What's so funny?

That hopeless attitude of yours...
...always so refreshing.

Madam! We weren't expecting you back so soon.
The meeting went smoother than expected.
How has Seraphina behaved while I was gone?

She's changed quite a bit.
She spends the entire day locked up in her room...

...and only leaves during meals.
Hm, is that so?

TOP 10 FASHION TRENDS
Buffering Please Wait...
Hm, that's weird...
PLACE

Something wrong with the router?
Never had connection problems before...

OPEN
?!

Mom, you're back?
Seraphina, give me your phone.
I thought I told you to remove those horrid extensions.
Wh-why?

Wasting time on boys and games...
Is this how you behave at school too?

You're becoming just like your sister!
Such a disgrace.

Mom! Leilah never did anything wrong.

PASS
Your phone!
...

Use these remaining three weeks to **carefully** reflect on what you've done...
I've shut off your Wi-Fi, so no distractions!

NO!
And keep your door open from now on.

SIGH
OPEN
That's strange.
John
[12:55:45 AM] *** Call ended ***
Friday ---
[05:23:57 PM] *** Call from Sera ***
[11:35:23 PM] *** Call ended ***
Sera - offline
Dad - busy
Saturday ---
[05:41:24 PM] *** Call from Sera ***
[02:09:57 PM] *** Call ended ***
Sunday ---
[3:12:09 PM] *** Call to Sera ***
She's usually online by now...
Wonder where she went.

I guess I'll play a quick round of AngryPigs while I wait!
click
click
click
click
click
click
click

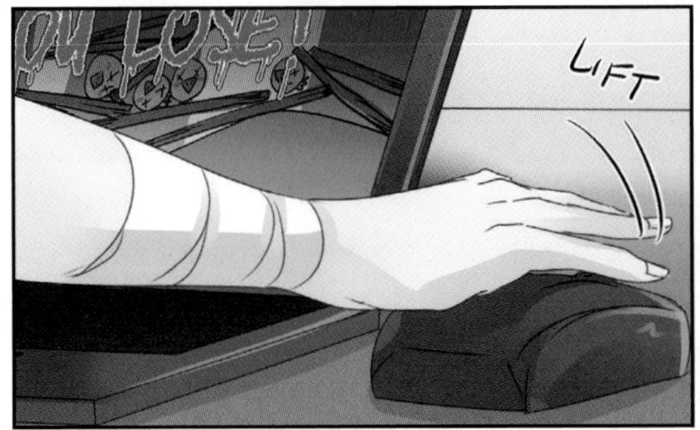

Is it really impossible to go any further?

HEY, LOSER!

READY TO LOSE YOUR LUNCH?!
WHAM
ACK!
TRIP

DRIP
OWOWOW! HOLY SH*T WHAT THE F*CK?
Step

I'm not in the mood for any bullsh*t today.

Order is natural.
The weak cower in fear of the strong.
Those with similar statuses get along.
And the strongest among us fight to rise to the top.
Everyone has their rightful place in society.
That's why a hierarchy is natural.
Because people naturally gravitate to where they belong.
OPEN
EXCEPT HIM.
A weakling without fear.
Where does he belong?
That look... He's definitely different.
Similar to that photo from two years ago.
John, is this who you **really** are?

What are you doing up here?
I should be asking **you** that question.
This area is for **Royals** only.
Commoners like you shouldn't be up here.

You need to leave.
I'm here to eat my lunch.
TAT
TAT

SIT

Maybe you didn't hear me.

This is where I always sit.

This guy's attitude...
Seriously throws me off...

You really aren't afraid of anything, are you?

Well, what's there to be afraid of?
You?

Of course.
I could crush you in an instant.
Lean

But you won't.
And what makes you think that?

Only sh*tty low-tiers would ever go after a zero.

What could a **King** like you possibly **gain**–
Satisfaction.
GLARE

Please. There's no satisfaction in destroying idiots who are much weaker than you.

How would you know?
Hmph.
crouch
You think you understand me, huh?
Then let me ask you this.
There's this one person I know, with no credentials.
Yet he walks where I walk, and sits where I sit.
The way he talks back to me especially ticks me off.
If you were in my position, what would you do?

SLURP
You should be grateful.

What?

If you can keep all but **one** person in line...
...then you're doing your job right.

What's he talking about?
After all, a **King** is nothing if his subjects refuse to follow him.

UP!
Welp, I finished my lunch.

?!
TAT
TAT

What's up with this guy?

Not a single one of my threats fazed him.
The only people with that kind of confidence...
...are those who stand at the top.

John...
...what were you at your former school?

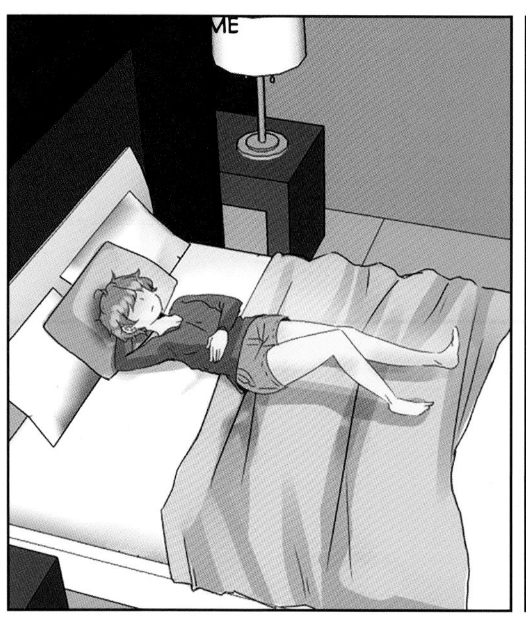

Miss. Please return to your workstation.

SIGH
What are those books for?
They are today's assignments.
You are to read through these...

...and write a report by the end of the day.
Give

But I just did that last night!

Sorry, miss. These are your parents' orders.
...

Scribble
Ugh...

The last time I **willingly** did this much extra work...

...was almost a year ago.

Back then, I put all my energy into the most trivial things...
I failed to take the time to understand myself.

Aw, not again!
This will be a three-part project, and I'll be assigning you each a partner to work with.
SMASH!
Why did I do that?
That wasn't like me at all.
What was it about **him** that made me act like that?
Each pair will be analyzing a specific set of books, and-
OPEN
Sorry I'm late!
I was at the infirmary.
Doc's Note
Yes, I can see that...
Please have a seat, John.
Pissed

As I was saying...
...you'll be pairing up and analyzing three books in total.
For each book, you and your partner will present your findings to the class.
Your final grade will be based on your presentations.
Now, the pairings.
Auriel and Elaine.
Blyke and Isen.
John and Seraphina.
??!!!

You may use the rest of class to sit with your partner and discuss your plans.
You've gotta be kidding...
GLOOM
Get your elbow off my desk.
What, you'll beat me up again?
Go for it.
But I'm your **partner**. So if you kick my a$$ now, I won't be able to help with the project.
Umm, **NO**.
If you don't, then I'll-
Oh don't worry, you're **not touching** this project.
Excuse me?
I can't have you ruin my perfect grade, so I'm doing the entire thing myself.
I'll provide you notecards for the presentation, so you'll read off those.

Think you can handle that?
...The hell?
I came here to learn! Not to-
Looks like it's been decided.
STAND
WHAT ARE YOU TALKING ABOUT?! WE HAVEN'T DECIDED SH*T!
Yes we have.
Tsk!

John.
Here are the notes I wrote up for you.
It's very straightforward.
Just read off the cards and follow my cues.
...
RIIIP!
HEY! WHAT ARE YOU DOING?!

I already told you, didn't I?
I came here to learn, **not** to freeload off you.
Since we had no communication, I went and did the entire thing too.
So, I won't be needing your notes.
All right, everyone, please settle down!
Presentations will begin shortly!
John and Sera, you're up first.
The book we read is called *Hamlot*. It's a tragedy written by Speareshake.
Maybe this won't be too bad.
This story contains a few main themes.
He got into Wellston without an ability, after all...
He must have some brains at the very least!

Before exploring further into these themes...
...John will give a quick explanation of the plot.
NOD
I'll give him this chance.
OH! My turn!
This story is a mystery surrounding the death of a King.
Okay, so far so good.
It turns out that the Queen had been conspiring with the new King all along,
and the entire death was planned.
Her son goes on a crazy rampage, pois
Wait, what?
That's not what happens at all...
He got the second half all wrong!
We are going to fail!

How did this happen?
B-
The grade distribution was good!
Class average was a B.
Not bad for the initial presentation!
Dis like the best score I've gotten since coming here!
Keep up the great work, everyone!
THUMP!
Seraphina? Where are you going?
Library.
?
...Huh?
What's up with her?
Did you hear? Seraphina got a B- on that presentation!

chatter
What? She did **that** badly?
Ugh, I know! I was so disappointed when I heard.
chatter
So much for being perfect, right?
Did you know she blew up at her partner in the caf because he wouldn't listen to her?
She's losing it. Girl can't even control a zero. Sheesh!
Next thing you know, we're gonna lose Turf Wars.
Some **Queen** she is! Why even look up to her?
*So this kind of thing happens **here** too, huh?*
*Because she's **Queen**, people are watching everything she does...*
I don't like her hair.
It's impossible to escape judgment.
chatter chatter
This kind of pressure is enough...
*...to push **anyone** over the edge.*
clench

If I get two 100s in a row, I can still get an A.
Hey.
...
Let's start the next part of the project.
If we work together, we'll do better.
SLAM!!
THMMP!!
That's not for you to decide.
Listen to me, John.
If you don't agree to use my notes...
...I'll send you to the infirmary **every day**, so that you won't even have a choice to work on it.

You would go **that** far for a perfect grade?
Yes.
Why? Do you **like** doing all this extra work by yourself?
Or are you trying to impress everyone around you?

That's none of your concern.
Well, I'm still not doing it.
If you beat me up, I'm gonna bullsh*t my half of the presentation, and we can both fail it.
Fine. Then I'll make the rest of your time here a living nightmare.

I'm a zero. How could you possibly make my life more miserable?
...
Why are you so stubborn?

I'm offering you the perfect deal.
We don't have to speak to each other, and we both walk away with an A!
Just do what I say!
No.
I don't care if you're a million times stronger than me.
Before coming here, I already decided that I'm gonna live the way I **want**.

WELLSTON LIBRARY
He's delusional.
MCBETCH Speareshake
TAT TAT
Why are you at my table?
Doing the project, obviously.
I already told you to not work on it.
And I told **you** that I'm doing my part!

So annoying.
So bossy!
Why'd I have to get stuck with you?
Phew! Finally done with that act.
Time for a break!
Yeah, right!
Let me see what you've done so far.
What?!
It's only reasonable.
I let you work on the project. You let me look over your work.

U-uh...I don't think you're qual–
What is this mess?
It's my summary!
Stop doing that!
This is almost entirely inaccurate.
You don't even have the plot figured out?
Stupid.
SWIPE
Well, the language they use is wacky.
And I don't understand it, okay?
Then ask!
Don't just make stuff up.

We put a lot of time into this presentation.
We practically spent the entire week in the library.
I explained everything to him in detail.
So, why...?

Ugh, what is it?
All that work paid off! We actually got an A!
What are you talking about?
It's not an A. Check it again.
Looks like an A to me.
You idiot! That's a minus! It means we suck!
Why are you always so negative?
Shut up!
Don't talk to me anymore!

Haha, look at this guy!
Who do you think you are?
Butting into our conversation like that!
You two should stop talking about others...
...and worry about yourselves.
Oh, please! We'll talk about whoever we want!
Seraphina's an embarrassment!
And she calls herself a role model?
No, you're **wrong**!
Who cares what she does, or what grades she gets?
We all know she's the most dedicated student here! So don't discredit her!
Is he defending me?

SHUT UP ALREADY!
SMASH!!
Blah blah blah. Keep rambling, you loser!
Like I give a damn about what **you** think?
You're just a waste of space.
WHAM!

EEK!
Ugh... What the-?
SERAPHINA?!
Don't touch my partner.
A-ah! I'm so sorry! I-I didn't mean to!
You didn't mean to?
What about everything you just said?
A-ah! I was only kidding!
I take it all back!
Get lost.
Y-yes, right away!
Come on. Let's get to work.
Umm... infirmary first?

WELLSTON LIBRARY
Seraphina.
I don't understand what this part means...
SLIDE
Can you explain it to me?
STARE
Huh, weird.
What?
Didn't expect you to actually ask me a question.
Hey, I want us to do well, okay?
So here, they're talking about how much they like each other...
NOD
Hm... Oh, I see! That's how these parts connect!
He's been surprisingly diligent these days.
What's gotten into him?

Good morning, class!
You'll be presenting the final part of your projects today.
Please take a minute to sit with your partners and discuss before we start!
What's wrong?
You're gonna burn a hole through the floor if you keep staring like that.
I just really want to do well today.
I don't like what everyone says about you.
So I won't drag you down anymore.
A bit late for that, don't you think?
Ugh!

Hey. Don't think about that anymore. Focus.
Ah...
Seraphina and John...
...please start us off!
I will give you this, though...
You are, by **far**, the most persistent person I've met.
Come on.
Let's get this thing over with.
Julio and Romiette
I'm not sure what it was...
He kept his facts straight...
But something happened that made him act differently...
...and never went on tangents.
We never spoke over each other either.

I'd say we did well.
Thanks.
Here you go, dear.
Thanks, Teach.
gulp
...
No way...
We pulled through!
We got the A!
John.

WE DID IT!
GRAB!
You gotta be happy about **this**!
I say we celebrate!
Drinks on me!
We may have gotten an A this time...
...but our overall grade was still an A-.
Aw, come on.
We both worked really hard!
That, itself, deserves a reward!
Uh, I'd rather go to the library...
Nope! You're coming with me, Seraphina.
You need to learn to relax every once in a while!
Ever had boba?

I don't know how he managed to drag me along.
Maybe it was because deep down,
I really wanted to celebrate too...

It's so ironic.

The first time I'd ever decided to reward myself was for something imperfect...

an A-.

I think this was when I began to realize reputation isn't everything.

I should focus less about how others perceive me, and more on what makes me happy.

Because in the end, I have to live with myself.

John,
you are truly extraordinary.

Even as a zero, you are able
to push through others' prejudice...

and stand up for yourself.

Even though you're at the bottom,
you can break molds.

You're an inspiration.

You showed me that even the "weakest" person has something valuable to offer.

That no one *is worthless.*

Miss.

Miss Seraphina.

Oh, it's you.

I'm not sure who you're expecting. Sorry to disappoint.
I'm here to collect your work.

I haven't finished yet.

I see.
I'll let your parents know.
Oh, your father wanted to inform you...
He's arranged for you to meet with one of his business partners for an internship opportunity.

NXGen Research Facility.
You have an interview scheduled tomorrow.
Tomorrow? That's short notice!

Miss...you've been complaining a lot since your return.
Perhaps all this time away from home...
...has softened you?

I will be back in an hour to pick up your assignment.

Please work efficiently.

SIGH
...

Every day has been the same painful grind.
Wake up.
Go to school.
Get beat up.

And come home with nothing to look forward to.

Why?

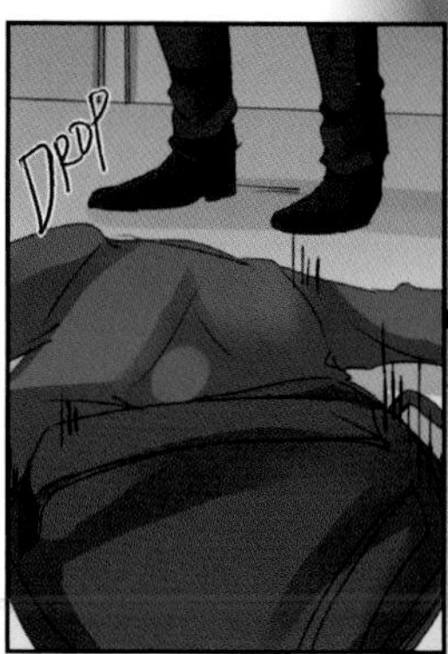
DROP

Why do I have to put up with all this?

WORTHLESS!
WHAM!

BAM!!
WHAM!
THEY'RE ALL WORTHLESS!
The weaklings with no backbone, who can't stand up for themselves!
The "elites" who waste their influence on the most insignificant things!
The mid-tiers who abuse their power with every chance they get!

BAM!!
EVEN... THE ONE PERSON I BELIEVED IN.
EVERYONE IS WORTHLESS!
BAM!!!
SHOCK!
Stop

huff
huff

Sera - offline
Dad - available
[6:48:29 PM] ***
[10:45:32 PM] ***
Tuesday ---
[6:14:04 PM] John:
Wednesday ---
[5:32:49 PM] John: hullo?
[6:23:58 PM] John: sera?
Thursday ---
Still offline?
It's been a week since we've spoken.

Where could she be?
What should I do?
Calling ... Dad
Hello? John?
Click
Hey, Dad.

What's up–
Hm, why're you calling from your laptop?
Something happen to your phone?
Um, I accidentally dropped it down a flight of stairs.
Well, that sucks!
I'll transfer some money for a new one, then.
Dad

Hey, Dad...
Could you send me another copy of *Unordinary*?
...
You know I can't do that.
My editor destroyed all my remaining copies.
Don't you have your own?
Why do you need another one?

John, is everything all right over there?
GRAB
John
Everything's fine.
I gotta go now. Still have a lot of homework to finish.
Call from Dad ... ...
WAIT, JOHN! DON'T HANG UP ON M–

CLICK

chatter
chatter
Chatter
Chatter
chatter
!!

Arlo, I don't know **what** you're doing but...

...he is...
TAT

...starting to show his **true** colors.

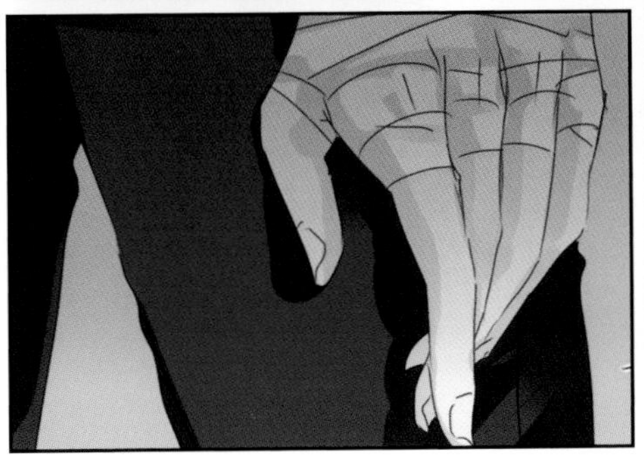

KNOCK
KNOCK
Come in.
Sorry I'm late.
That's quite all right, Keene.
Please have a seat.
Last night, authorities found yet another dead body, this time in the town of Wellston.
NOT CROSS. DO NOT CROSS
NOT CROSS. DO NOT CROSS.DO NOT CRO
The victim was identified as Shatterstack, another well-known superhero.
His body was branded with the picture of a flame, the logo of the infamous EMBER.
This murder follows the usual profile of EMBER's victims: high-tier vigilantes. Reporters are wondering...
...with the deaths of all these high-tiers, why the authorities haven't escalated their investigation?

What are your thoughts?
Hm...
It's frightening... to see another high-tier die.

What is EMBER trying to accomplish with all these murders?
Are they trying to frighten the rest of us?

Regardless, defeating a high-tier is not easy.
Each of us is like a one-man army.

Keene. Do you remember **Rei**?
He graduated three years ago.

Of course!

He was **King** before Arlo stepped up.
A brilliant student with so much potential-
He was killed by EMBER last month.
?!
W-what do you mean?

How's that possible?
He got his hands on a copy of *Unordinary*.
Such a waste of talent.
Just what kind of powerful backing does EMBER have?
To be able to take out Rei just like that...

Wellston has the highest concentration of high-tiers, so we should take caution.

I want you, as Head of Security, to monitor every person who enters the school until this EMBER nonsense is over.
I'll tell the rest of the staff to keep their eyes open as well.
Yes sir.

With Seraphina's suspension, and now, Rei...
That's two cases related to *Unordinary* linked to Wellston.

Yes.
I have a feeling the authorities will want to keep an eye on us from now on.

If you sense any spies roaming around campus, flush them out and bring them to me for questioning.
I don't want the authorities meddling into my business.

TAT

Wonder what he's up to...

SHOVE
What are you glaring at, idiot?

Don't touch me.

PFTT!
Hahaha. "Don't touch me," he says?
That new haircut of yours must be messing with your head!

Don't forget who the strongest one here is.

I CALL THE SHOTS!

SO I'LL DO...
...WHATEVER I WANT!

Disgusting!

GRAB!
PAH!
Huh?

ACK!
SLAM!!

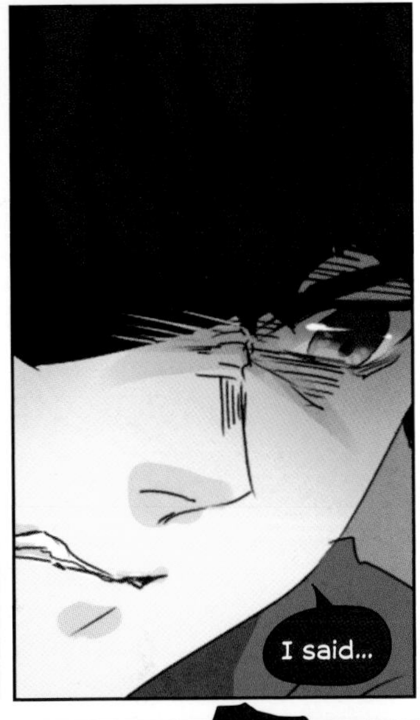
I said...

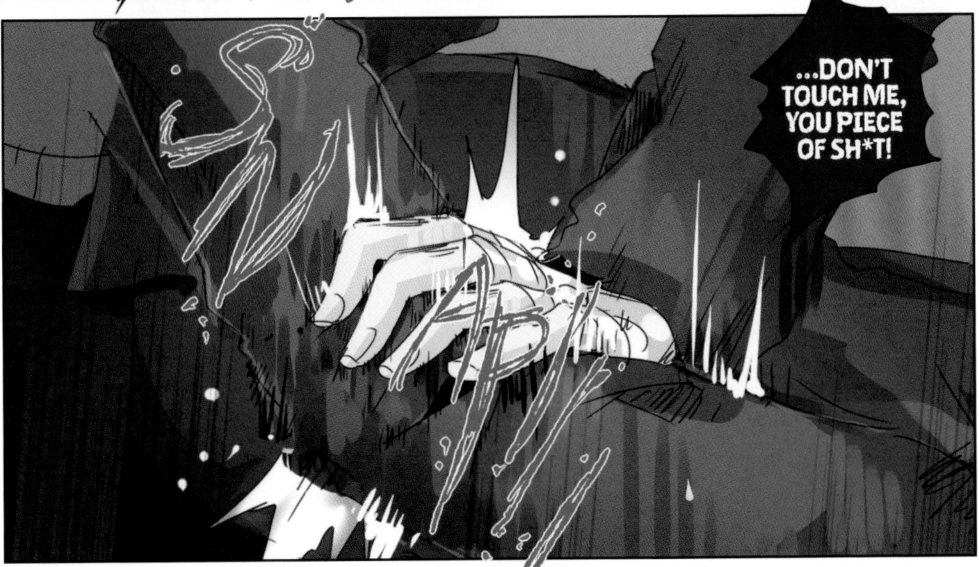
...DON'T TOUCH ME, YOU PIECE OF SH*T!

!!!
AUGH! MY ARM!
GET OFF OF ME!!
HEY! LET GO OF HIM!
You stupid zero!

GLINT

STAND

Hmph.
Did you really think that by rallying a bunch of people...
...you could take **me** down?
Claire.

I thought you had more foresight than that.
After all, you knew long before we met...
SNAP
...that I was going to become King.
Isn't that why you helped me in the first place?
So that you could use me to further yourself?
Well, you succeeded, and I played right into your hands.

What more could you want?

...

GRAB!
ANSWER ME!!
WHY DID YOU TURN EVERYONE AGAINST ME?
ACK!

WHY WOULD YOU BETRAY ME LIKE THIS?!
DO I REALLY MEAN NOTHING TO YOU?

HAVE YOU SEEN YOURSELF?!

LET GO!
SHOVE
SMACK!!

YOU'RE ALWAYS LOOKING FOR REASONS TO HURT!
TAKE A GOOD LOOK AT WHAT YOU'VE BECOME!
YOU'RE SO CONCEITED!
YOU DON'T CARE ABOUT ANYONE BUT YOURSELF!
YOU TYRANT!

YOU HYPOCRITE!
ALL THIS STRENGTH YOU HAVE NOW...
YOU DON'T DESERVE ANY OF IT!
What...?
I NEVER SHOULD'VE HELPED YOU!
I WISH I'D NEVER MET YOU!
SHUT UP!!
MAKE ME!
GO AHEAD AND BEAT ME UP LIKE YOU DO WITH EVERYONE ELSE!
SHUT UP!
I SAID...

Monster.

ARGH!!
CRACK!
!!
She's overpowering me so easily!
loosen
A direct hit from her and it's game over.

OOF!
WHAM!

!!

BAM!
BOOM!
He's the only one blocking my escape!
If I take him down quickly, then–

Better watch your back.

STRIKE

?!
SURPRISE, MOTHER F*CKER!
WHAM!!

His arm...
THIS IS PAYBACK FOR HITTING ME EARLIER, A$$HOLE!!
SLAM!!
COUGH
Hahaha!
NUDGE
GRAB

Look at how pitiful you are!

Not so tough now, are we?

HUFF
I can't focus...

HEY, ZERO! HE ASKED YOU A **QUESTION!**

ANSWER HIM, NOW!

BAM!

GUSHHH!!
WHAT?!

WAAAAHHHHHH!!!
THROB

Illena!!

AUGH!
flop

Are you all right?
This stupid barrier just appeared from nowhere!

Barrier?!

A-Arlo!
TAT TAT

Ah, sorry you had to witness this mess...
You see, this zero was annoying us.

Tch!

We just wanted to teach him a little lesson...

You know, like, put him in his place!

U-um, what's this for?

A-Arlo?

He keeps shrinking it on me!
At this rate, I'll be crushed!

Who gave you the right to speak?

Your eyes were just glowing.
You have the power to fight back...
So why would you rather be beaten to this extent?

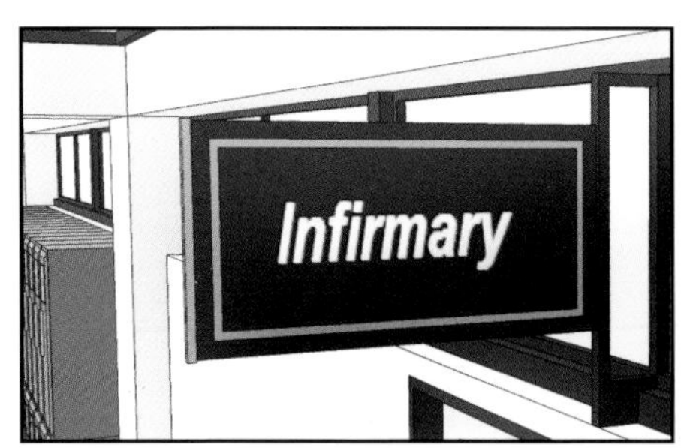
Infirmary

MBER STRIKE
ANALYSIS by Isen
Hm...
Isen wrote the top story again. Not bad.

RUMBLE
J-John...
What is it, Adrion?
Erm... I-It's, uh...
QUIT STALLING ALREADY!
AND SPIT IT OUT!
GRAB
Ah... sorry!
I-It's about Claire.

I overheard her talking to the Jack...
She said the only reason why she approached you that day...
...was because she had a vision, long before, of you climbing to the top.
And because you were so weak and isolated at the time...
...she wanted to get to you first.
That way you'd trust and rely on her.
Is this some kind of joke?
N-no! I heard it with my own ears!
SHUT UP!
WHAT THE HELL ARE YOU TRYING TO SAY?!
SMACK
THAT EVERYTHING I'VE BEEN THROUGH WITH HER WAS FAKE?
BULLSH*T!

Please calm down, and I-listen!
She's been using you this whole time!
She had a vision that you'd be overthrown!
They're gathering behind your back as we speak!
You need to be careful!
BE QUIET!
I DON'T WANT TO HEAR IT!
BAM!
UGH!
...
YOU LIAR!
John! I've been behind you since day one!
I'd never lie to you!
Right now, you're blinded by your own ego!
Open your eyes!
If you keep letting things go on like this...
...you're gonna lose **everything**!

Hah, good one.

Did you forget how powerful I am?

FLINCH
I'LL NEVER LOSE...
...BECAUSE EVERYONE ELSE IS TRASH!

NOW GET THE HELL OUT OF MY SIGHT!

?!

Look who finally woke up-

WHAM!

WHY DID YOU HELP ME?!
WHAT ARE YOU PLANNING?
WHAT'S YOUR MOTIVE?
GRAB!

Don't be so full of yourself.

I don't know what kind of delusional world you're stuck in...
PUSH
...but not everything revolves around you.

Take a good look at who you just hit.

!!
Luckily for you, I'm very patient.
Unlike **some** people, I don't act on impulse.

STAND
You should know...

Uh...
...I **despise** people who refuse to learn their place.

Next time, I won't be so lenient.

What am I doing?

shut

Beep!

Isen has been following you.
5 seconds ago

I saw it.
GLINT
And Arlo saved him from those guys...
...which means he probably knows about it too.
PFFF
SPEAK OF THE DEVIL!
ISEN.
Freeze

UGH, DAMN IT.
Just the man I was looking for.

O-oh, hey Arlo!
Didn't see you there!
What's crackin'?

You're still spying on John...
...even after I told you to drop it?
I dunno what you're talking about...

Don't try to hide it.
I **know** you're looking for another story for the newspaper.

Um... n-no!

BREAKING NEWS!
School zero turns high-rank!
NONONO!!!
SHUSH, ARLO!
Squeeze

Please keep it down!
If anyone from the club hears, they'll steal my story!

Hm. How about we make a deal then?
Huh...?
As if I had a choice!

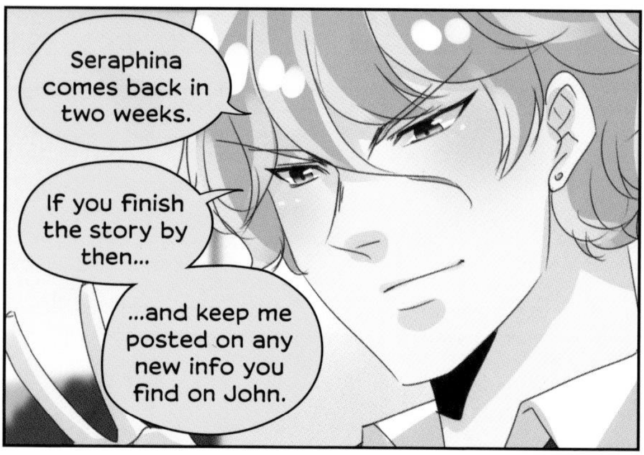
Seraphina comes back in two weeks.
If you finish the story by then...
...and keep me posted on any new info you find on John.

I'll **guarantee** you a front-page article.

All right, man!
You got yourself a deal!
Fwp

Good.
Don't disappoint me.

WAVE

What did I just agree to?

WELLSTON DORMITORIES

TAK
TAK
TAK
TAK
TAK

NEW BOSTIN
FOUND YOU, BABY!
Your old school transcript!
TAK
TAK
EXPELLED

TAK
TAK
HUHUHUHUHUHUH
I'll track you all the way back to your roots!

Hey! Congrats on top story this week!
WHATCHA UP TO?
ASFAAS! BLYKE!

GAWD! EVER HEARD OF PRIVACY?!
??
But this is the common area...

...

Why are you so obsessed with that John guy?

He's a total a$$!
Remi tried to help him, and he lost his sh*t and slapped her.

Oh, I heard about that.
Hm, instead of worrying about John...
...why not spend more time with her?

Since Rei passed, she still hasn't been herself.

I'm worried for her, you know?
Mmhmm.
Hey, man, can you at least pretend to care?
SHE'S YOUR FRIEND TOO!

Okay, fine!
Let's take her out this weekend.
You have a place in mind?

I dunno, the mall?
Get her mind off recent events...
Hm, that could work!

All right, I'll let her know, then.
Don't bail on us this time, okay?
Don't worry, I won't.
Where was I?

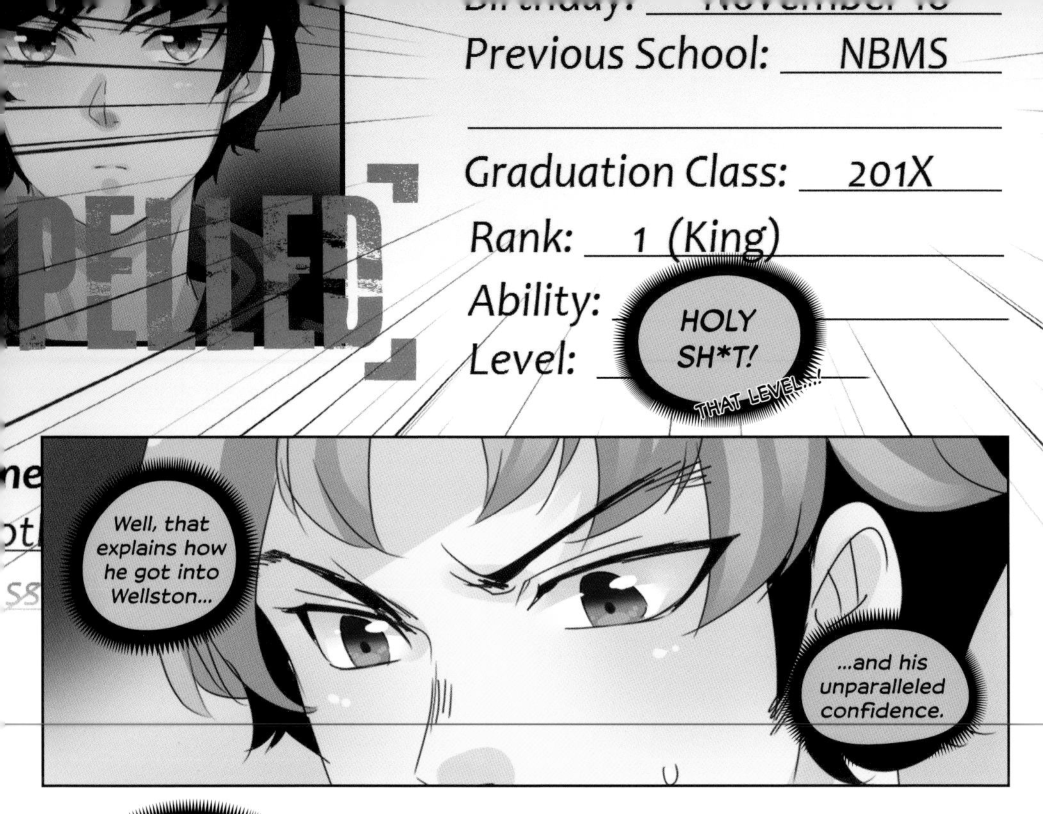

Previous School: NBMS
Graduation Class: 201X
Rank: 1 (King)
Ability:
Level:
HOLY SH*T!
THAT LEVEL...!
Well, that explains how he got into Wellston...
...and his unparalleled confidence.

Hm, it says he was expelled two years ago as a second-year.
The timing doesn't match up!
He transferred into Wellston last year as a second-year.
EXPELLED

Maybe he took a year off in between...?
What was he doing?
And how could any school even **think** of expelling him?
WITH POWERS LIKE THAT!
TAK
TAK

Comments: Average student; does not ge
with others; does not like to participate in class; h
aggressive/violent tendencies. NOTE: Do not activate
ability when handling situations involving John .
lsion during second year for excessive violence
"Excessive violence"? How?
click
pg 1
This guy **single-handedly** took down half his class...
...for an **unexplained** reason?!
He's not someone to mess with!
If we expose him, who knows what he'll do?

UNORDINARY

EXTRAS

Only first-years at Wellston are allowed to play dodgeball in gym class.
Older students are stronger, making these games too destructive for school.
Oh, yeah!
DODGE THIS!
Algebra
TOSS!

SLAM!!
Eek!
Welp, she's down.
Are you okay?
ELAINE OUT!

Hehehe, YES!
Got another one!
I'm sorry guys...
It's okay, Elaine. You did great!
Isen, we gotta come up with a strategy.
Yeah. What should we do?
?!
SHOOOM!

DODGE!
DAMN IT!
He pulled a fast one!
I can't dodge both at the same time!

ISEN! NO!
BZZZZT!!
UGH!
SSS
You good?
Yeah, nice save!

Hey, you can't do that!
And why not?
Because this is **dodgeball**!
I don't see you dodging!
You almost shot Isen's face off!

TOOT!
Okay, listen up!
No more shooting, and no destroying the balls!
I don't get paid enough for this...

Tsk!
Hey, Seraphina!
Aren't you gonna help me?
...
IGNORED
TOSS
Algebra

Hey quit throwing it at me?
We're on the same team.
Oh, so you **are** paying attention!

BAM!
ACK!
WHAM!

They got me...?
What's that you said about paying attention?
SHAD-DAP!
Blyke, you're out! Get off the court!
STOMP!
STOMP!
Hmph!

Great job!
SLAP
YES!
Guess I'm up.
Hold this for me.
GRAB

TOSS!!

WHAA

Looks like we have a winner!
Couldn't have done that sooner?
...
If I had done it sooner...
...then nobody else would get to play.

...

Good point.

Can I have my book back?
O-oh, yeah.

Teach, I believe I've fulfilled my physcial requirements for the day.
May I go to the library now?
Go ahead.
Thank you.
TAK
TAK
Uh...are they okay?
TAK
Bonus story: Dodgeball [end]